A ROYAL LOVE MATCH

Then Clive walked down the stairs and Alissia went with him.

She held his hand all the way down the stairs.

When they reached the front door, he bent down, and picking Alissia up, kissed her on both cheeks.

"You are a very brave and lovely young girl," he sighed. "I do so hope when you are a little older we will meet again."

Alissia put her arms around his neck and hugged him.

"I am so glad that Nanny was so clever and saved you by putting Mama's cap on your head."

"And you gave me your hair, Alissia. As I think it has brought me luck, I am taking it away with me in my pocket as a very special keepsake of a very special young lady."

Alissia giggled.

"I like to think of you doing that."

"I will put it away in a safe place and if I am ever in trouble again, I will expect you to come and save me."

"I would love to," answered Alissia coyly.

He kissed her on the cheek again.

Then he swung himself onto his horse.

THE BARBARA CARTLAND PINK COLLECTION

Titles in this series

A ROYAL LOVE MATCH

BARBARA CARTLAND

Barbaracartland.com Ltd

THE BARBARA CARTLAND PINK COLLECTION

Dame Barbara Cartland is still regarded as the most prolific bestselling author in the history of the world.

In her lifetime she was frequently in the Guinness Book of Records for writing more books than any other living author.

Her most amazing literary feat was to double her output from 10 books a year to over 20 books a year when she was 77 to meet the huge demand.

She went on writing continuously at this rate for 20 years and wrote her very last book at the age of 97, thus completing an incredible 400 books between the ages of 77 and 97.

Her publishers finally could not keep up with this phenomenal output, so at her death in 2000 she left behind an amazing 160 unpublished manuscripts, something that no other author has ever achieved.

Barbara's son, Ian McCorquodale, together with his daughter Iona, felt that it was their sacred duty to publish all these titles for Barbara's millions of admirers all over the world who so love her wonderful romances.

So in 2004 they started publishing the 160 brand new Barbara Cartlands as *The Barbara Cartland Pink Collection*, as Barbara's favourite colour was always pink – and yet more pink!

The Barbara Cartland Pink Collection is published monthly exclusively by Barbaracartland.com and the books are numbered in sequence from 1 to 160.

Enjoy receiving a brand new Barbara Cartland book each month by taking out an annual subscription to the Pink Collection, or purchase the books individually.

The Pink Collection is available from the Barbara Cartland website www.barbaracartland.com via mail order and through all good bookshops.

In addition Ian and Iona are proud to announce that The Barbara Cartland Pink Collection is now available in ebook format as from Valentine's Day 2011.

For more information, please contact us at:

Barbaracartland.com Ltd.
Camfield Place
Hatfield
Hertfordshire AL9 6JE
United Kingdom

Telephone: +44 (0)1707 642629
Fax: +44 (0)1707 663041
Email: info@barbaracartland.com

THE LATE DAME BARBARA CARTLAND

Barbara Cartland who sadly died in May 2000 at the age of nearly 99 was the world's most famous romantic novelist who wrote 723 books in her lifetime with worldwide sales of over 1 billion copies and her books were translated into 36 different languages.

As well as romantic novels, she wrote historical biographies, 6 autobiographies, theatrical plays, books of advice on life, love, vitamins and cookery. She also found time to be a political speaker and television and radio personality.

She wrote her first book at the age of 21 and this was called *Jigsaw*. It became an immediate bestseller and sold 100,000 copies in hardback and was translated into 6 different languages. She wrote continuously throughout her life, writing bestsellers for an astonishing 76 years. Her books have always been immensely popular in the United States, where in 1976 her current books were at numbers 1 & 2 in the B. Dalton bestsellers list, a feat never achieved before or since by any author.

Barbara Cartland became a legend in her own lifetime and will be best remembered for her wonderful romantic novels, so loved by her millions of readers throughout the world.

Her books will always be treasured for their moral message, her pure and innocent heroines, her good looking and dashing heroes and above all her belief that the power of love is more important than anything else in everyone's life.

"All the most beautiful paintings and sculpture, all the most inspiring poetry and all the most uplifting music comes from only one source and that is Love."

Barbara Cartland

CHAPTER ONE
1651

The nursery was filled with sunshine.

Nanny was sitting at the table ironing the ribbons that decorated the nightcap her Mistress wore at night.

Seated in the bay window, Alissia, aged nine, was making a drawing of flowers from the garden that were prettily arranged in a vase in front of her.

She intended to paint a particularly special picture as a birthday card for her mother who she adored.

Elizabeth Dalton, however, was not very strong and she had to spend a great deal of time in bed.

She was sleeping at this moment, which was one reason why Alissia was upstairs with Nanny.

They had already been out for a walk in the garden, enjoying all the beautiful flowers and planning a surprise for her mother's birthday.

Their house was on the other side of the river Avon from Pershore, a village in the County of Worcestershire, famous for its large Abbey.

Elizabeth Fenwick had lived there all her life and when her father died the estate became her inheritance.

It was only a few months before his death that she met Bruce Dalton who was roving around England.

She was to learn later that he was a Scot.

He was, although no one was aware of it, reporting back to Scotland concerning the strength and location of Oliver Cromwell's Regiments in the South of England.

However, when he first saw Elizabeth he lost his heart – as well as his ambition to undermine Cromwellian rule.

In the House of Lords in 1649 the Monarchy had been abolished and Cromwell's Army had forcibly ejected a large number of Members of the Long Parliament from the House of Commons.

And early that year the King of England, Charles I, had been tried by Parliament and executed in London.

It was two years later that Oliver Cromwell was named Lord Protector.

With Scotland subdued and largely in the hands of the all-powerful Ministers of the Presbyterian Kirk, he set about trying to give his Government a civilian rather than a military aspect.

Bruce Dalton found himself increasingly popular with the people of Worcestershire and he learnt that many of them wanted to bring back the Stuarts who they looked on as their rightful Rulers.

As soon as Elizabeth became engaged to him, her father died, leaving her the house and the estate on which she had been brought up since she was a baby.

Bruce was frightened now he was happily married that his identity would be discovered by the Cromwellian troops as they were always nosing about looking out for trouble.

He had called himself Bruce Dalton and it was in that name that he was married to Elizabeth.

He was, however, although it would have been a great mistake for anyone to find out, the second son of the Earl of Dalwaynnie.

The Earl was known to be an admirer and supporter of the Stuart Kings and it was essential, if Bruce was to remain in England, that no one should find out that he was his father's son.

He was completely and blissfully happy with his beautiful Elizabeth.

The only sorrow was that they only had one child, Alissia, who was now nine years of age.

Their family life was very quiet and there had been no obvious difficulties to overcome.

Bruce had been so happy he had almost forgotten his beloved Scotland.

Soon the supporters of the Stuart King in Scotland decided to seek the restoration of Prince Charles, the only son of Charles I, now aged just eighteen, to the throne in London.

They had recognised Charles Stuart as their King in Scotland immediately after the execution of his father.

Bruce had been sent moving descriptions of him from his relations,

"*He is a tall man – dark, slim and graceful,*" they wrote. "*He is charming to meet and we are all thrilled by his courage.*"

They finished by saying,

"*We are determined that he should be recognised as our lawful King, and you must help us, dear Bruce, in every way you can.*"

They wrote more fully to him month by month.

Prince Charles had agreed to sign the Covenant, swearing to establish the Presbyterian Kirk in England.

He had arrived in Scotland in April 1650, managing to avoid the ships of the Commonwealth and landed at the mouth of the River Spey.

The news of Prince Charles's arrival had made the Council of State in London determined to invade Scotland before a Scottish Army could march into England.

Nine months later Bruce received a letter to say that the Prince had been crowned Charles II at Scone near Perth on 1st January 1651.

It was where all the Kings of Scotland had been enthroned for centuries.

Finally Bruce was informed that in July the Prince was marching South with an Army of thirteen thousand men, English and Scottish, to lay claim to his inheritance.

While Bruce was still wondering what he should do about it, the Prince had advanced as far as Worcester.

Bruce had managed in the last few years to become friendly with the local supporters of Cromwell.

But now he was in a dilemma.

Every drop of his Scottish blood told him that he should join up with Prince Charles and fight for him as he would have done had he been in Scotland.

But Elizabeth was ill and could not leave her bed.

His beloved Alissia was only nine.

How could he leave them alone and unprotected to join Prince Charles at Worcester?

Yet he knew it was what he should do.

While Bruce was worrying over this problem, torn by his love for Scotland, his own country, and yet tied by his position in England, the battle started.

Prince Charles understood, Bruce knew, that he was seriously outnumbered by the serried ranks of the Army of the Commonwealth.

'What on earth am I to do? What the devil am I to do?' Bruce asked himself a thousand times.

Yet he knew, however much he loved Scotland, his duty lay with those who were dependent on him, his wife Elizabeth and his daughter Alissia.

*

Upstairs in the nursery the maid, Mary, brought in the afternoon tea on a tray.

"Is there any news, Mary?" asked Nanny eagerly.

Mary put the tray down on a side table and started to lay a cloth over the table where Nanny was working.

"They're all sayin' as things be very bad," replied Mary. "And the men be praying that Prince Charles will escape 'cos if 'e's taken prisoner there's no doubt they'll kill 'im like they killed 'is poor old father."

She spoke with a bitterness that made Nanny look quickly towards Alissia.

Then she said to Mary in a whisper,

"Be careful what you say. Children have long ears and, if they're questioned, it's best they don't understand the danger of what they says."

Mary nodded to show that she understood.

Then putting the tray down in front of Nanny, she went out of the room.

"Come and have your tea, Alissia," called Nanny.

"I've very nearly finished drawing these flowers," answered Alissia, "and when I paint them I do hope Mama will be very pleased."

"I know she will, and you paint very well indeed, dearie, she'll be right proud of the card you're makin' for her birthday."

"I wonder what Papa will give her," Alissia mused, getting up from her seat by the window and walking across the nursery. "Last year he gave her a gorgeous brooch and she was very very pleased with it."

"Of course she was, and I would expect she'll have somethin' even prettier this year."

Nanny started to pour out the tea for herself.

Alissia had a cup of milk and helped herself to the honey sandwiches that cook had made for her.

"If Mama was well," said Alissia, "we could have a lovely party. But Papa told me last night he thought she was too weak for one this year."

"She must take great care of herself. I'm sure in a day or two she'll be sittin' out in the garden and then you can paint some of the flowers there when you're with her."

"She must not see my birthday card until Monday," insisted Alissia.

"No, of course not," agreed Nanny.

As she spoke the door opened and Mary said in a voice which sounded strange,

"The Master says you're to 'ide this 'ere gentleman, Nanny, and 'e says that Cromwell's men are not far behind 'im."

Nanny jumped to her feet.

Coming in through the door was a man wearing the uniform of a Scottish soldier.

He was in a dishevelled state and there was blood running down over the fingers of his left hand.

He was a young man and not much older, Nanny guessed, than eighteen or nineteen.

He was very tall and good-looking and seemed to tower above Nanny as she exclaimed,

"You're wounded, sir!"

"It is really only a slight scratch," the young man answered. "But my horse was shot from under me. I am Clive More. I have managed to escape, but I don't think *they* are far behind me."

6

"Then come in here, sir," Nanny urged, opening the door of her bedroom. "Undress quickly and get into that there bed."

He then hurried into the bedroom and Nanny turned to Alissia.

"Run down to your mother's room," she asked her. "Don't tell her what's happenin', but bring me up the face-powder she puts in the drawer of her dressin' table."

Alissia did not argue or ask any questions.

She merely did as Nanny told her and ran quickly down from the nursery, which was on the second floor, to the first floor where her mother's bedroom was situated.

It was a large room with windows looking out over the garden.

As Alissia quietly opened the door she could see that her mother's eyes were closed.

She was asleep in the big bed with its canopied top and white muslin curtains falling down on either side.

Alissia tiptoed over the room to the dressing table.

Opening the drawer she found the face-powder that her mother used sparingly, but she always wanted to look as lovely as her husband told her she was.

The Scottish soldier had said Cromwell's men were not far behind him, so Alissia knew that every minute was crucial as she ran back up the stairs.

She was most intelligent for her age.

She knew that the battle that was raging outside the City of Worcester was of great significance.

Not only to her father but to England, but she had been warned that it was something she must not talk about when there were visitors in the house.

Before reaching the nursery she looked out of the window on the way up the stairs.

She saw coming up the drive there were a number of men on horseback and they were wearing the uniform of Cromwell's Roundheads.

So she hurried back into the nursery and opened the door into Nanny's bedroom.

Clive More was already lying in Nanny's bed and Nanny was just finishing bandaging his arm.

"There are soldiers coming up the drive, Nanny," murmured Alissia.

Nanny pulled all the bedclothes over the stranger's arm and took the face-powder from Alissia.

Then much to Alissia's surprise she put it down on the bed.

She pulled the lace nightcap she had been mending over the young man's head and tied the silk ribbons under his chin.

She then powdered his face.

Clive More was already looking pale from losing so much blood and the white powder made him look rather strange, but certainly less like a soldier.

Nanny finished tying the ribbon into a bow under his chin.

Then turning to Alissia, she urged her,

"Come here, dearie."

Alissia obeyed.

Nanny then picked up the pair of scissors that were lying on top of the bed.

She cut off one of the curls of fair hair that fell over Alissia's shoulders.

Alissia was surprised, but she did not say anything.

She merely looked on as Nanny twisted a piece of cotton round the curl.

She pushed the end of the hair under the nightcap and arranged it carefully against the cheek of the man lying in her bed.

Next Nanny cut off another of Alissia's curls and arranged it against his other cheek.

It certainly made him look far more like a woman than a man.

"Now keep your eyes shut," she whispered to him, "and appear to be fast asleep even if they speaks to you. Do you understand, sir?"

"I understand and thank you so much," the young man mumbled.

He spoke in a low voice, but Alissia thought it was a very pleasant one.

Nanny pulled the blinds down halfway and taking Alissia by the hand she drew her back into the nursery.

"Sit down at the table and eat your tea as if nothin' has happened, dearie, and if they asks you any questions, you're too shy to answer them. Do you follow me?"

"Yes, Nanny, I understand. They must not capture that man in your room or they will kill him."

Nanny did not answer.

A few moments later the door opened and two men walked aggressively into the room.

Nanny then turned round and stared at them as if she was astonished at their sudden appearance.

Alissia merely looked up holding a honey sandwich in her hand.

"Has a soldier just come in here?" one of the men asked abruptly.

He was obviously an Officer.

He looked disreputable and mud-splashed as if he had been riding hard over dirty roads and fields.

"There's no one here except me and the children," Nanny responded. "Would you like a cup of tea?"

"I haven't got time for that," he replied roughly.

He was looking round the room as Nanny spoke.

He even peered under the nursery table as if he thought someone might be hiding there.

Then he walked to the door which led into Nanny's bedroom.

"If you're goin' in there," Nanny said to him in a sharp voice, "don't you go wakin' Miss Lucy. She's got a bad cold and is runnin' a temperature. I've only just got her off to sleep."

It was the voice of authority which the soldier must have recognised from when he was a child.

"I'll be as quiet as a mouse, I promise, Nanny – "

He opened the door and peeped in.

He had no idea that Nanny was holding her breath, while Alissia was watching wide-eyed.

They heard him move across the room and open the wardrobe.

It only contained Nanny's clothes and he closed it quietly.

Then he came out of the bedroom shutting the door behind him.

"You can't say I was anything but real quiet," he said, "and your young charge is sleeping peacefully."

"I suppose I should thank you," declared Nanny. "But you've not told me who you're lookin' for."

"I reckon it's only polite to tell you," the Officer answered. "It's the son of the Marquis of Morelanton and we'll find him sooner or later wherever he may be hiding himself."

"Poor young fellow, whatever has he done to hurt you?" Nanny asked scornfully.

"You know the answer to that," the Officer smiled. "He wants to put another of those Stuarts on the throne and we've had quite enough of *them*."

He moved to the door as he spoke and as Nanny did not say anything, he added,

"Goodbye, Nanny, I'm sorry to have disturbed you, but when we catch young Charles Stuart and finish off all those who're supporting him, everything will be peaceful again in the land."

Nanny did not reply.

The Officer was joined by the man with him and they went out closing the door behind them.

Nanny and Alissia heard their footsteps going down the stairs.

Only when there was silence did Nanny give a deep sigh of relief.

"Will they go away now?" Alissia asked Nanny in a frightened voice.

"We can't be sure of it, dearie, until we hear or see their horses goin' down the drive."

"I want to go to Papa," Alissia piped up.

Nanny shook her head.

"It might make things awkward for him. You stay here with me, dearie, till he sends for you."

She rose from the tea table and opened the door of her bedroom.

Clive More was still there lying motionless where she had left him in the bed.

"That was a near thing," he said in a voice that was almost inaudible. "Thank you more than I can ever say for being so brave and saving my life."

"You stay where you be," insisted Nanny. "We're not safe until we're certain they've left the house. Is your arm still hurtin' you? I'll give it a proper bandage when I'm quite certain no one's peepin' in at us."

"Only a Nanny as brilliant as you," Clive sighed, "would have ever thought of passing me off as a sick girl."

"They're a real nasty lot if you asks me. So what's happened at Worcester, then?"

"I only hope the Prince has escaped," he replied. "Actually I must not stay here – making things dangerous for you."

"You would be stupid if you left before the battle at Worcester is over and the soldiers go back to London."

"I am very afraid we are defeated," Clive groaned. "I only hope and pray the Prince will be able to escape."

"Well, I'll go and see what's happenin' downstairs. Alissia will stay here with you and, if anyone else comes upstairs, pretend to be asleep.

Clive looked at Nanny.

"I always used to do exactly what my own Nanny told me to do," he grinned.

Nanny smiled.

"Those are my orders and don't you try any tricks till I comes back," she added with authority.

She went out of the room leaving the door open.

Alissia could go back into the nursery if she wanted to, but instead she sat down on the side of the bed.

"Was it terribly frightening when you were fighting the battle?" she asked him.

"To tell the truth," he replied, "it was incredibly frightening. But I don't want to talk about it. Tell me what you do here and if you have a nice pony to ride."

"*A lovely pony*. He is called Lightning and I have had him for more than three years and I can go very very fast on him."

"That is just what I was doing when I was running away with several others from a mob of horrible soldiers who wanted to kill us."

"But you escaped – "

"Very fortunately because my horse was so fast," was his answer. "But there were two men concealed in the wood at the bottom of your drive and they shot my horse so that it threw me."

"I am sorry, very sorry. I would be very unhappy if they shot my pony."

"I loved my horse," he told her, "so you know how I feel now that I have lost him."

"But you are lucky they did not kill you too."

"I know that, Alissia, but they would undoubtedly have taken me a prisoner if your Nanny and you had not been so clever and I want to thank you both very much."

Clive then smiled at her and she thought how funny he looked with her curls on either side of his face – and her mother's lace nightcap on his head.

A few moments later when Alissia was still telling him about her pony, her father came into the room with Nanny.

"They have gone now, Clive," he said to the young man in the bed. "It was very astute of you to find your way to us here in Pershore."

"My father told me that this is where you lived," Clive replied, "and I was hoping to have the chance when we were in Worcester to meet you. But I did not expect it to be under such terrifying circumstances."

"Terrifying indeed," Bruce Dalton agreed. "They have ridden away and I have convinced them that I am on their side and will inform them if any Scot dares to come here asking for help."

He thought that Clive looked horrified and added,

"I live here, and it would be a great mistake for anyone to think that I am a Scot or anxious to rid England of Cromwell. You might have been on the way to victory."

"I wish I could tell you that was so," Clive replied, "but they outnumbered us and we were overwhelmed."

"And what about the Prince?" Bruce Dalton asked almost in a whisper.

Clive shook his head.

"I can only hope he escaped, but the fighting was vicious and I had no idea what was happening until I found myself just outside the City and being attacked ferociously by the Cromwellians."

"We will just have to wait and hope that the Prince has escaped," Bruce remarked wistfully.

*

It was actually not until nearly three days later that they discovered the worst.

The Scottish Army had been totally overwhelmed at Worcester and a great number of their soldiers had been killed and the rest taken prisoner.

It was by a miracle that the Prince had managed to escape in disguise after the battle through the Northern gate of the City of Worcester

No one knew where he was.

It was not until a long time later that Bruce Dalton was informed that he had made his way to Boscobel in Shropshire and there he had been welcomed at the house of a Roman Catholic family.

In their grounds he had hidden in an oak tree, whilst the whole of Southern England was searching for him.

He was described by the vengeful Cromwellians as,

"That despicable, malicious and dangerous traitor Charles Stuart, son of the late Tyrant, a tall black man over two yards high."

There was no response to this from the people of Pershore, who were only extremely grateful that the Battle of Worcester had not extended as far as their town.

They were not really interested in the price of one thousand pounds on Charles's head – in point of fact the high reward did not tempt the English at all into looking for him.

It was not until much later in the year that Bruce learnt what had actually happened.

The Prince, disguised in rough country clothes, his long curly hair cut short and crammed under a greasy old hat, had made his way to the Sussex coast at Brighton.

It took him six weeks to reach Brighton and from there he had been carried in a fishing boat to Fécamp in Normandy.

"I thank God for that," Bruce had exclaimed when he heard the news.

When he told Alissia, she had jumped for joy.

"I am glad, so very glad!" she cried. "And that nice gentleman, Clive, who came here will be glad too."

"He has gone back to Scotland, my dear, and if he is wise he will stay there. We will not be rid of Oliver Cromwell for a long time, I am afraid."

*

As the years passed by, Bruce had his own troubles.

Elizabeth's weakness grew far worse and she spent most of her time in bed.

Only occasionally did she feel well enough to come downstairs and sit in the garden with her daughter – or in the window near the big fire in their comfortable drawing room.

Finally, five years after the Battle of Worcester had seemed to be almost forgotten, Elizabeth died peacefully in her sleep and Alissia, now aged fourteen, had to cope with her distraught and miserable father.

"We were so happy together," he kept saying, "how could she leave me and how, my darling daughter, can we manage without her?"

Because he was so perturbed, Alissia had unwisely encouraged him to go to London to visit some of his old friends.

She thought that maybe he would forget for a while the happiness he had had with his beloved wife.

She had naturally not anticipated in any way what would eventuate.

Because Bruce was feeling so incredibly lonely, he instinctively turned to other women for comfort.

Although Nanny was still with her, Alissia now had a middle-aged Governess who came to the house every day from Pershore to give her lessons.

She also had a teacher of music and the Vicar of Pershore Abbey instructed her in history in which he had excelled when he had been at University.

It was not the same, however, as having her father with her.

When she heard that he was returning home again after another of his long visits to London, she felt thrilled and delighted.

At first he had come back home every month as he considered it his duty to see to the estate and to catch up with Alissia.

Then his absences had extended to two months at a time – and then a little longer.

Nanny and the servants, who had been at the house ever since her parents married, looked after Alissia.

Occasionally she played with other children of her own age and Nanny would arrange a party for them and in return Alissia was asked back to their homes.

One day she had a letter telling her that her father was coming back for good and her heart leapt.

She was so excited at the news that she could think of nothing else – her darling Papa was coming back to her at last.

But only when that letter was followed by a second did she realise that the reason he was returning was that he had married again.

"You will, my dearest," he wrote, *"of course never forget your beloved mother.*

But you will find that Lady Hester Gordon, who is to become my wife, will make you much happier than you are at the moment, as she has made me."

"I would never have thought that Papa would marry again," Alissia confessed to Nanny.

"If it comes to that, nor did I, dearie, in fact I thinks he'd never find another woman to take your dear mother's place."

Alissia could not help feeling too that it would be impossible.

Her father arrived back home with his new wife and Nancy Gordon, her daughter from her previous marriage.

From the very moment she arrived, Alissia knew that Nancy was jealous of her.

She clearly resented that Alissia was undoubtedly prettier than she was.

Nancy was quite a nice-looking girl, but Alissia had in recent years grown more and more like her mother, her golden naturally curly hair being her crowning glory.

Her truly English pink-and-white complexion made the vivid blue of her eyes seem all the more striking and even Nanny praised her at times,

"You look real pretty, dearie, and that be the right word for it. If you're not a success when you grows up and go out into the Social world, I'll eat my hat!"

It was one of Nanny's favourite expressions and it always made Alissia laugh.

"I should hate you to have to eat your hat – it would taste horrible!" she laughed. "So, Nanny, help me to look exactly like Mama."

"She was a real beauty, make no mistake," Nanny would say.

Then to amuse Alissia she would arrange her hair in one of the more fashionable styles that could be seen in Worcester in certain quarters for the odd callers who would occasionally came to see if her father had returned or was still in London.

When her Papa did return, everything was different.

Lady Hester professed every intention of enjoying herself and that meant she needed an audience, preferably of men to admire her constantly.

She did not at first think of Alissia as a rival for her daughter, but Nanny became aware of it and did not hide her feelings.

Then as time passed and Alissia grew even more lovely, Lady Hester began to look at her in a very different manner.

She was always disparaging her and finding fault with everything she did, but fortunately Alissia's father did not listen to her.

That his daughter looked so like his first wife made her perfect in his eyes in whatever she did or said.

So he merely ignored the sharp remarks which his new wife contributed to the conversation.

Alissia was, of course, only a schoolgirl.

She was still receiving lessons from her various teachers, so it was natural to leave her behind when they went to parties and it was only when her father insisted that she accompanied them.

*

Then suddenly in 1658, when Alissia was only just sixteen, everything changed.

At first no one in Pershore was that interested when they discovered that Oliver Cromwell, the Lord Protector of England, was in ill health.

They heard various reports of his illness, but even when these became increasingly frequent, no one seemed much concerned.

Then at the end of August an extraordinary gale hit the country.

It swept across England and the locals believed it was a warning from God.

Trees, even huge oaks, were uprooted and the roofs were blown from houses and ships were sunk at sea.

Church steeples fell, crashing down into the streets and people were swept off their feet and characteristically the English saw the havoc of this gale as a warning of still more disasters yet to come.

"Ye mark me words," an old man in Pershore said, "there be real trouble after this. Hell on earth, I shouldn't wonder!"

Alissia felt sad when her favourite lilac and acacia trees crashed to the ground. Some big oaks fell across the drive and had to be cut up with a great deal of trouble and expense.

Oliver Cromwell died on the 3rd September 1658 and his successor as Lord Protector of England, his son Richard Cromwell, became known as 'Tumbledown Dick' and was described by everyone as totally unfit to rule in his father's place.

He was summarily dismissed from his office by the Army after only six months and an arrangement was made to settle his debts on condition he left England for Paris.

Just as soon as he had departed, the Army dissolved Parliament and a Committee of Safety was established to control the country.

But the situation in London became unstable.

Finally General Monck, who was in command of the Army in Scotland, made up his mind to come South to end the disorder and summon a new Parliament.

It was immediately and inevitably decided to recall Prince Charles from exile.

He had been crowned King Charles II in Scotland in 1651, and was now declared King at Westminster early in May 1660.

On his birthday, 29th May, King Charles arrived in London.

The Army brandished their swords and shouted out with inexpressible joy.

His way was strewn with flowers.

Bells rang and the streets were hung with tapestries.

Fountains ran with wine.

The Lord Mayor, Aldermen and Members of the City Companies wearing their fine liveries with chains of gold, together with most of the Nobility, greeted him.

Music was heard in all the streets and many stood in the Strand and blessed God.

Without a single drop of blood being shed, the very Army that had rebelled against him was now welcoming him back in a fantastic manner that took his breath away.

It was a Restoration that had never been witnessed in history before.

And it opened a new life not only for King Charles II but for all the people over whom he reigned.

CHAPTER TWO

When the news reached Pershore, the Abbey bells were rung with enormous gusto.

People then covered their windows and doors with pieces of coloured paper or material.

Flags appeared in the streets.

It was then that Alissia's stepmother, Lady Hester, firmly declared,

"At least we can now go back to London where we belong."

Her husband looked at her in surprise.

"London?" he queried.

"Yes, of course, Bruce. Don't be so stupid," Lady Hester replied. "Nancy is nineteen and has had no chance until now of meeting anyone of importance, you can hardly want her to be an old maid."

"Which is not very likely at nineteen," he answered her somewhat feebly.

"Well I have no intention of staying here, Bruce, when after all these years everything exciting is happening in London."

"But we have nowhere to live when we arrive there, my dearest."

"I will soon find somewhere. If you would like to stay here and arrange for someone else to manage the farm, I will go ahead myself to London and do all the dirty work of finding somewhere for us to live."

Bruce replied rather limply that it would be all too much for her – and of course she should not travel alone.

But Lady Hester was insistent.

The whole house was turned topsy-turvy while she decided what she and Nancy would take with them – and what would have to be left behind.

"Naturally you can bring us whatever else we may require later, but I intend to take quite a number of items with me I know I shall need and the sooner I can find a really comfortable house in a fashionable part of London the better."

It was obvious that she was not including Alissia in her plans, but her father had no intention of leaving his adored daughter behind.

It was several more days before he realised that his wife had now decided it was perfectly safe for them to reassume his ancestral title – the Earldom of Dalwaynnie.

She had already informed the servants that in future they were to address him as 'my Lord'.

Bruce had learnt with sorrow only a year ago that his father had died and now his elder brother, of whom he was particularly fond, had been killed while fighting in the Scottish Army.

"In point of fact to be honest with you I am rather ashamed of myself," he murmured to Alissia. "I was safe and happy here in our lovely home, but after your darling mother died I suppose I should have become a Scot again."

"You helped your country when you could, Papa, and I am certain that the secret reports you sent to Scotland were of great use to the Royalists."

"I did my best, Alissia, but at the same time I feel rather guilty about using my father's title only now, when he did everything in his power to bring King Charles back to the throne."

"As indeed you did too in your own way," Alissia chipped in. "Anyway, Papa, it is a mistake to always be looking back. Now we have to look forward. Stepmama is right about that."

"Well you must really enjoy yourself in London at any rate, my darling. You have never been there and I will have a great deal to show you. I was always very fond of it as a City when I was a young man."

It became more and more clear that her stepmother was making every effort to leave Alissia behind.

"Nancy and I will go on ahead," she persisted, "and find a house. Then, of course, Bruce dearest, *you* must join us."

It was perfectly obvious that she was not including Alissia.

But after a moment Bruce merely commented,

"If you take the best carriage, I am wondering what Alissia and I will travel in."

"I thought perhaps you would come on horseback," replied Lady Hester. "I know you would never wish to be parted from your beloved horses."

There was a little pause and then she added,

"Alissia can come later. I am sure we can arrange for someone coming from Pershore to give her a lift."

There was silence for a moment before Bruce came back firmly,

"Either I have a house with all my family in it or *I stay here!*"

His eyes met his wife's.

She realised that he was serious and it would be a mistake to continue arguing with him.

"Very well," she conceded, "so I will be expecting you and Alissia. At the same time you must not come too soon in case I encounter difficulties in finding exactly what I require."

Lady Hester and Nancy departed for London in the very best carriage and Alissia and her father were left alone together in the house.

A week later he was visited by a Scottish lawyer who had travelled South to see him.

"I was half afraid, my Lord," he began, "that you would have left here and gone to London, everyone I know is travelling there for the Coronation and I quite expected to find an empty house on my arrival."

"I am waiting to hear from my wife when she finds the right accommodation for us," responded Bruce, "but I imagine that every hole and corner will be filled to watch the King crowned in glory!"

The lawyer laughed.

"I bring you good news, my Lord, and you will find it will be easy to afford the accommodation you need now that you can well afford to pay for it."

He handed Bruce an account of the assets that had been accumulated by his father over the years.

When he read it he was absolutely astounded that there was so much money left in his father's estate – in fact it was more than double his expectations.

He was now, as the Head of the family, a very rich man indeed.

"I am very much hoping, my Lord, that you will be coming to Scotland soon," said his visitor. "There are so many of your Clan who remember you as a boy and who wish to see you again before they leave this world."

"And I would like to see them," agreed Bruce.

It certainly made life much easier for him now he had so much money.

So he set in motion the improvements he wished to make on his estate in the country and he realised he could afford what would be considered suitable accommodation for his family in London.

However, he was a Scot.

And he thought it would be a mistake to let his wife spend every penny she could take from him on clothes – or on entertaining people who she considered would be useful to them socially at Court.

However he did recognise that Nancy and Alissia must make new friends and be known to the social world and that was a major obligation the moment King Charles arrived back in London.

Bruce had heard various stories of the vast amount of entertainment that was already taking place in London and he was certain that his wife and Nancy would want to be in the thick of it.

Equally he had to think of the future.

He had already told himself that he was happier in the country than he could ever be in a City and as soon as possible he would return to Pershore.

Realising that this was what her Papa was thinking, Alissia did not like to disillusion him.

Nancy and her mother had never for one moment stopped complaining that the country was so dull and that there were no important people to entertain.

Worcestershire had never been, they pointed out, a County where many aristocrats lived and they quoted the Counties around London with large houses, inhabited by ancient families who had always been a part of London's social life that extended all the way to the Throne.

"Now that our King Charles is back," Lady Hester droned on, "we will stand a chance of meeting our relatives as well as the social figures who have helped to govern our country in the past. They have created the correct Society into which I would hope Nancy will marry successfully."

Without her saying so, Alissia knew this meant she wanted a title for her daughter at least as significant as her own.

One thought often occurred to her, although she had been too tactful to say so.

It was that Lady Hester would never have married her father if she had not learnt that secretly he was the son of the Earl of Dalwaynnie.

She had admitted once that he had confided in her because she knew some of his relations.

Alissia was alert enough to calculate that from that moment Lady Hester clung on to him and finally she lured him into offering her marriage.

Alissia had to admit, however, that her father was not as lonely or unhappy as he had been at first when her mother died.

He was undoubtedly very fond of Lady Hester.

At the same time he was not in love with her as she remembered him being in love with her Mama – their eyes would light up when they saw each other.

The moment he came into the house after being out in the grounds he used to call out her name and they never spoke to each other without a soft caressing note in their voices.

Alissia knew this denoted *love*, a love which came from their hearts and souls and had been blessed by God.

She was well aware that this note was no longer there when her father spoke to his new wife.

'If only Mama had lived,' she mused to herself, 'how different it would all be.'

But she knew it would be a mistake to say anything to her father.

She had made no protest when Lady Hester swept off to London in the family's very best carriage drawn by four magnificent horses with Nancy in her smartest clothes sitting beside her, and with some of the servants following behind in another vehicle.

Alissia knew there were a great number of items in it which Lady Hester had removed from the house.

And they actually belonged to her as her mother had left most of them to her in her will.

But she thought it would be most inappropriate to make a scene about it as it would only upset her father.

However, she had a suspicion that the collection of miniatures Lady Hester had chosen to take with her were valuable – as were a number of pieces of silver from the safe.

They and the pearls which her mother had always worn might easily be sold.

She did try to tell herself that her stepmother was only taking care of them in case there was a burglary, but at the same time she resented anything that had belonged to her mother being removed from the family home.

As soon as Lady Hester and Nancy had gone, her father began making sure that the estate continued to run the way he wanted when he was to be absent in London.

Fortunately most of the workers had been with him for many years and they were all men he could trust and who he knew would not stoop to steal from him.

He commented to Alissia,

"An estate, like an Army, needs someone to lead it. If I am not present, I am frightened things may go to rack and ruin."

"I am sure they will not happen, Papa, although we may have to live in London part of the year, we can always come back here in the spring so that you can organise the planting of the crops."

Her father had smiled at her.

"You are so right, my dearest. That is exactly what we will do, unless, of course, you have fallen in love and married some handsome and charming man who will make you even happier than your poor old father has managed to do."

"You have made me very happy, Papa, and I love being here. Like you, I do rather dread starting a new life in London that will be so entirely different from the one we have always loved so much in the country."

"How do you know I dread that?" he enquired.

"I can see it in your eyes and hear it in your voice, Papa, but if London is really disappointing and we are both unhappy, we can come back here. After all the house will be well looked after by the old couple you are putting in as caretakers, and I know that Jason is thought to be the best farmer in the neighbourhood and will be an excellent part-time manager."

Yet, when eventually the letter came from London that they were to join her stepmother immediately, Alissia knew that her father was saying goodbye to the country with tears in his eyes.

Lady Hester of course was now called the Countess of Dalwaynnie and she was correct in asserting that her husband should be in London with her for the Coronation.

She had written to say with glee that she had met His Majesty the King.

She had told him how much Bruce had done for him when he had been abroad in exile and of his secret reports to Scotland on the activities of the Cromwellians.

King Charles wanted to reward everyone who had supported him and he had therefore offered Lady Hester Apartments in the Palace of Whitehall until she was able to find a house that suited her.

The Coronation was unusual in that the King paid a great deal of attention to the wishes of the populace.

On the eve of his Coronation, the King took part in the traditional procession from the Tower of London to Whitehall.

It was officially described as a 'spectacle', pleasing to the people and actually followed the same route as for the mediaeval Kings such as Richard II.

Needless to say the procession meant an early start and all the dignitaries were told they were to be mustered on Tower Hill at eight o'clock in the morning.

They were also told, which Alissia found amusing, that their mounts were not to be 'unruly or stinking.'

Alissia and her father were delighted by the idea of riding in the Royal procession, but the new Countess of Dalwaynnie and Nancy complained bitterly as neither of them were good riders.

Alissia in fact enjoyed the Coronation more than anything else.

As the Foot Guards of the King passed them with their red and white feathers on their heads, she applauded them strenuously.

She felt perhaps that they had suffered terribly in the last years – more than those who could afford to escape the Cromwellians and avoid suffering under their harsh regime.

The triumphal arches under which the King passed were intended to represent the Crown emerging from its hiding-place.

One that delighted Alissia most depicted a woman dressed to represent a rebellion. She wore a crimson robe crawling with snakes and held a blood-stained sword in her hand.

At every turn on the road it was emphasised that the King stood for stability and for the social order which had been neglected for so long.

The best arch and the one which thrilled Alissia the most was supported by a woman who addressed the King with the following words,

"Great Sir, the star which at your happy birth

Joy'd with his beams at noon, the wandering earth

Did with auspicious lustre then presage

The glittering plenty of this golden age – "

A great deal of money had been spent on replacing the regalia that was essential to every Coronation – much of it had disappeared or been melted down during the rule of Cromwell. In fact the total cost of replacement was over thirty thousand pounds.

The Coronation demanded an unceasing changing of clothes for the King and most of it was made of Cloth of Gold.

The King's golden sandals with high heels made him tower over the Bishops and Nobles around him and the ceremony required that he should wear a series of mantles of crimson velvet trimmed with ermine.

Even his trousers, his breeches and stockings were made of crimson satin, and rich golden tissue embellished the chairs of State.

There was a horse whose saddle was embroidered with pearls and gold and a large oriental ruby was provided by a jeweller named Gomeldon.

A further twelve thousand stones were needed for the stirrups and bosses and these, however, were only lent for the occasion.

In addition scarlet cloth was used in abundance in St. Edward's Chapel and on the benches in Westminster Hall and Westminster Abbey.

Everything possible contributed to the impression of magnificence.

But it all, down to the silk towel held by the Bishop before the Coronation Communion, had to be paid for.

It was fantastic, at the same time really impressive and exciting, which was exactly the effect that the King desired.

Visitors from abroad were impressed to find that England was by no means the broken down country they had imagined it to be after the excesses of Cromwell.

No one could have failed to be seriously moved by the solemn and ancient Service in Westminster Abbey.

All the congregation held their breath as the Crown was finally placed on the King's head by the Archbishop of Canterbury.

Then a great shout rang out which seemed to echo and re-echo in the high roof.

Immediately after every member of the English and Scottish Nobility swore fealty to their Sovereign and then they ascended the Throne and touched the King's Crown, promising to support him with all their power and loyalty.

It was all the more moving in that they had waited for this moment for so long.

There were tears in Alissia's eyes and more than one aristocrat taking part was busy with his handkerchief.

To everyone's relief the weather was dry and sunny throughout the ceremonies.

These were rounded off by a mammoth feast held in Westminster Hall.

The Earl Marshall, the Lord High Steward and the Lord High Constable appeared riding richly caparisoned horses to attend the first Court of their new Monarch.

Even the humble clerks of the kitchen, who brought up the vast procession of servers, wore black figured satin gowns and velvet caps.

To Alissia's delight the King's Official Champion, Sir Edward Dymoke, was riding a white charger.

He made a grand entry preceded by trumpeters and throwing down his gauntlet he made the traditional and ancient challenge,

"If any person of what degree soever, high or low, shall deny or gainsay our Sovereign Lord King Charles the Second – here is his Champion, who saith that he lieth and is a false traitor."

This was all very exciting to those who were able to see it happening.

Thanks to the Countess's plea to the King, she with her husband and the two girls were given excellent seats in Westminster Hall.

Alissia had always been very interested in history and she could not help remembering that it was in the very same Hall some twelve years earlier that the King's father, Charles I, had been on trial for his life.

At long last King Charles II washed his hands in water ceremonially brought to him by the redoubtable Earl of Pembroke and a host of attendants and then having done so, he departed from Westminster Hall, as he had arrived, by a beautifully decorated barge on the River Thames.

This was indeed a most fitting conclusion to such a stirring parade of pomp and power.

It was all widely reported as not being in any way inferior in absolute magnificence to that of any Sovereign in Europe.

King Charles and the Duke of York later presented their Coronation robes not to a museum for posterity but to a theatre – they were to be used a few years later in a play by Sir William Davenant and later still in a performance of *Henry V* by Orrery.

When exhausted after such a long day, Alissia crept into her bed, she thought that it was a day she would never forget.

It seemed extraordinary that the years of fear were over.

And yet looking back she could see all too clearly the fear that had flickered in her father's eyes when the dreaded Cromwellians came to search their house in the country.

She often thought of the young man who had come into her nursery with his hand covered in blood and was so cleverly hidden by Nanny in her bed.

Every time she thought about him, she remembered how he had said goodbye to her and the way he had kissed her.

He had stayed with them for nearly a week until Nanny had said his arm was completely healed, and then her father had found out that the victorious Cromwellian Army had left Worcester for London taking their prisoners with them.

"Where will you hide yourself?" Bruce had asked Clive.

"I am going home," he had replied.

"To Scotland?"

Clive had nodded.

"There are only two possibilities left open to me," he answered. "Either I follow King Charles who I hope and pray will find his way back to France or I go North and stay in Scotland where I belong."

"Then of course my advice to you," said Bruce, "is to go to Scotland. Your father will need you."

"That is exactly what I think," replied Clive. "My elder brother, if he is still alive, is fighting with the Scots. My father will be alone in the Castle and will, I think, need me."

"I am sure he will," Bruce agreed. "Therefore you must be incredibly astute in making your way back without being caught."

He gave him money as Clive had only a little left in his pocket.

He also gave him rough clothes, which made him unnoticeable, to look like an ordinary young man from an ordinary family moving about the country.

When he bade farewell to Nanny in the nursery, he said,

"If you ever need help in the future, I hope you will find someone as kind as you have been to me. I know that I owe my life to you, and there are no words I can find to express my gratitude."

"Now you take real good care of yourself," Nanny replied briskly. "You're so right to go back to your father. It's Scotland where you belongs and if you will take my advice you'll stay there till King Charles, who you've been brave enough to crown at Scone, is on his rightful Throne in London."

"That's exactly where I hope he will be, Nanny."

In the drive outside waiting for him was the horse Bruce had given him.

Then Clive walked down the stairs and Alissia went with him.

She held his hand all the way down the stairs.

When they reached the front door, he bent down, and picking Alissia up, kissed her on both cheeks.

"You are a very brave and lovely young girl," he sighed. "I do so hope when you are a little older we will meet again."

Alissia put her arms around his neck and hugged him.

"I am so glad that Nanny was so clever and saved you by putting Mama's cap on your head."

"And you gave me your hair, Alissia. As I think it has brought me luck, I am taking it away with me in my pocket as a very special keepsake of a very special young lady."

Alissia giggled.

"I like to think of you doing that."

"I will put it away in a safe place and if I am ever in trouble again, I will expect you to come and save me."

"I would love to," answered Alissia coyly.

He kissed her on the cheek again.

Then he swung himself onto his horse.

"One day," he called to Bruce, "I will give you an even finer horse to replace this one. But you may have to wait until King Charles is back on his rightful Throne."

He lowered his voice as he said the last words and Bruce instinctively looked over his shoulder as if he was afraid someone might hear them.

Then he smiled and responded cheerfully,

"Good luck and give my love to Scotland!"

"I will certainly do so," Clive promised.

Then forgetting that he was not in his uniform, he saluted before he rode off.

Alissia thought of him often and could still feel his kiss on her cheek.

She hoped that she would see him when they came to London.

But she was not sure whether he had accompanied King Charles abroad or stayed in his own country where he belonged.

*

She and her Papa and Nanny had arrived in London only a few days before the Coronation took place.

There was not time for her to get to know the other people living in the Palace of Whitehall.

She only passed them in the corridors or saw them when they were hurrying down the stairs to dine with the King or to attend some other Royal function.

Now as she closed her eyes, she felt sleep coming over her almost like a soft cloud.

Yet she was thinking again that perhaps tomorrow she might see Clive again.

The next day, now that the Coronation was over, her Papa was not as busy as he had been since their arrival.

Alissia persuaded him to take her down to the river to see the barges arriving.

There always seemed to be a number of beautifully dressed women and smart men in the barges which drew up outside the great Palace of Whitehall.

She had heard that King Charles enjoyed playing the game of tennis – it was a game she had read about and heard about, but had never seen it played.

Earlier Royals had very much enjoyed tennis and King Henry VIII had excelled at it – and it was also a part of the Stuart family tradition.

Charles I had played it well and so had his nephew Rupert and in exile, Alissia had been informed, the Duke of Gloucester had become an expert – and it was jokingly rumoured that he contemplated earning a living at the game in the future if times were hard!

Bruce had learnt from his wife that King Charles played early in the morning, six o'clock being his favourite time.

"Even if I have to get up very early," said Alissia one day, "I would love to see him play. And it is a game I would like to play myself one day."

"Nonsense!" her stepmother had scolded her. "It is a game for men and certainly not for young ladies like you and Nancy."

She spoke repressively as she usually did to Alissia, but she remained determined to see the King play tennis, just as she wanted to have the opportunity of swimming, as he regularly did, in the Thames.

Apparently he really loved swimming, which he had enjoyed when he was in France and later in Holland and as soon as she and her father arrived in London they were told that the King always went swimming early in the morning.

"He will often rise at five o'clock," their informant said, "and go boating and sometimes swims just outside the Palace. At other times he swims with his brother James at Battersea, Putney or Nine Elms."

What Alissia discovered also about the King, which appealed to her more than anything else, was his passion for dogs.

A great sadness of leaving home was that her father thought that it would be a mistake for her to bring a dog to London – at least until they were certain that he would be acceptable wherever they were staying.

Alissia knew that he was actually thinking of her stepmother, who had made it very clear she disliked dogs and disapproved of Alissia having her favourite spaniel in her bedroom.

In fact the Countess became very unpleasant about it before she left for London.

Jimbo therefore had to be hidden in Nanny's room if there was any likelihood of her stepmother coming up the stairs.

Fortunately she did not often go anywhere near the nursery where Alissia had remained even though she was grown-up.

"I do love the nursery," she had always claimed. "I have all the things there that belong to me and I have no wish to move."

Nancy was established in one of the best rooms on the first floor, while Alissia remained on a floor higher up.

Her first sight of the King as soon as she arrived at Whitehall was of him striding along with a train of spaniels scampering and barking beside him.

She was to learn later that playing with his spaniels was the King's habitual method of whiling away the many hours of Government business that he found tedious and increasingly dreary.

The Royal pets, however, were not popular with the Courtiers and they believed, as the Countess did, that they were better outside than in, but the King's passion for his spaniels was known by everyone at Whitehall.

Alissia found herself becoming more and more an admirer of the King before she actually met him.

Now she felt sure that the King would want to see her father and she made him promise that if the King sent for him, she could accompany him into the Royal presence.

"It may not be possible," he asserted, "but I will do my best. I well know how much you admire him, as I do. Equally he is the King and a very great number of people demand his attention."

"If he gives his attention to those lovely spaniels I saw him with," said Alissia, "I am sure he will have time for me as well. And of course, Papa, he must thank you for helping to bring him back to his Throne just as he rewarded all those people at the Coronation."

She hesitated for a moment before she added,

"I thought you, Papa, should have the Order of the Garter."

"Thank you so much, darling, but I do not deserve it," her father replied. "In fact, if I am truthful, I ought to have served in the Scottish Army as my brother did."

"Then you might have been killed and you know, Papa, I love you very very much and I cannot imagine my life without you."

Her father was touched and put his arm round her and as he kissed her gently, she knew he was thinking of her mother and how much he had loved his first wife.

It was impossible for anyone, Alissia believed, to take her mother's place.

Either in her father's heart or in hers.

CHAPTER THREE

When he looked back, Clive, now the Marquis of Morelanton, reckoned it had been an incredible miracle that, after the terrible defeat at the Battle of Worcester, he had been able to escape back to Scotland.

The Cromwellians were all on the look out for stray Scotsmen making their way home.

As Bruce had given him an especially good mount, he managed to sneak out of the Worcester area without any undue trouble.

But as soon as the horse had carried him quickly out of the area of immediate danger, he decided he would be safer and less noticeable on foot.

He therefore sold the horse off cheaply to a small country dealer, who asked him no awkward questions on obtaining a bargain.

He deliberately avoided the West side of England down which the Scots had marched on their way South.

He slept under a hedge at night if it was not raining or in the very cheapest inns where a stray traveller meant money and was welcomed with open arms.

It took him very nearly three months to complete the journey.

Finally he reached home to find that his brother had been killed by the Cromwellians and his father was dying of old age and depression.

This left him with a great deal to do.

Firstly he had to pull the estate into good order, as it had run down somewhat while he had been away.

He began by introducing several new ideas that he had thought for some time were necessary as his father had disliked anything that was different from how it had been in his father's and grandfather's time.

It was in fact a pleasure that Clive had not expected to be able to give orders to his large staff and have them instantly carried out.

He learnt with overwhelming sadness how many of his clansmen had been either killed or imprisoned after the Battle of Worcester.

Naturally he was delighted to learn that eventually King Charles had reached France in safety.

Since he had been crowned King at Scone on his return to Scotland eight months previously, Clive, being a Scot, naturally thought of him as King, even though he was in exile.

Every day Clive had feared he would hear that King Charles had been captured or killed.

And because he had always been a great admirer of Charles, he felt certain that one day he would surely come into his own.

In the meantime the Cromwellians had lost face by letting him escape and so they vented their rage on those who had supported him and were now in their power.

While King Charles had certainly escaped against enormous odds – in fact it was considered a miracle that he had reached Paris in safety – England lay in the iron grip of Goliath.

This was Cromwell's nickname among the people.

On the very same day of the King's embarkation to France, the Earl of Derby was executed and had he been captured, Charles would undoubtedly have shared the same fate.

In the years that followed Clive learnt all he could of how his King was surviving in exile.

He was not in the least surprised when he was told that his resourcefulness, intelligence and sheer courage had made him a hero in Paris.

Clive, however, did not spend all his time worrying about his King.

Scotland was still in the grasp of the Cromwellians and there was great danger for any Scot if he so much as mentioned Charles's name.

Clive therefore set himself to work extremely hard on his own estate.

Because he was exceedingly handsome and as tall as Charles himself, it was not at all surprising that he was relentlessly pursued by young women.

Those who were married, when they looked at him, had an inviting expression in their eyes and actually for the next two or three years he indulged himself with several of them whenever he had the chance.

A regular flow of visitors would come to stay at his ancestral Castle and amongst them were attractive married women who were only too pleased to fall into his arms.

He also spent a great deal of time riding and often wondered when he would be able to replace Bruce's horse he had lent him for his escape with another thoroughbred as good if not better.

'He saved my life,' Clive often said to himself, 'and one day I must express my gratitude to him appropriately.'

On the death of Oliver Cromwell, and some twenty months later, the proclamation of Charles as the King of England, Clive's heart leapt.

He thought that now at last would be his chance to travel to England and pay homage to his King.

There was naturally great excitement in Scotland as soon as Oliver Cromwell was dead and the Scots thought that things would change dramatically to their advantage.

News would come from England regularly, but it was always out of date by the time it reached the people on the other side of the border.

Yet every word of it was of significance to Clive.

He read everything that he could find about King Charles and when he would be likely to return to his own country.

But there was some time to wait.

Finally, several days after the event, Clive learnt that King Charles had been rowed ashore at Dover in the Admiral of the Fleet's barge.

It was at about three o'clock in the afternoon of the 25th of May 1660.

He was followed by a good number of his friends and supporters in a smaller boat which included one of his dogs escorted by a footman.

Clive had smiled when he read that once he was on dry land Charles knelt down and thanked God for his safe arrival.

Clive did not miss any of the reports of the thunder of guns and cannons at Dover and that they had continued firing all the way on the King's progress to Tower Hill in London.

Just as bonfires sprang up from hill to hill and from town to town.

'If only I was with him,' Clive muttered to himself a thousand times.

He learnt that at Rochester the King had greeted the Army on horseback.

And it was on horseback that His Majesty saluted the Morris dancers who were gambolling on the heath.

And it was on horseback that King Charles finally processed through the Borough of Southwark.

Then led by the Army he crossed London Bridge.

To Clive every word he read about the reception of the King and the cheering crowds was almost as exciting as if it was happening to himself.

He was alone in his comfortable sitting room in his Castle, but his heart was with the twenty thousand people, who were laughing, shouting and crying because their King Charles had returned to claim his birthright.

Clive read that the streets of London were literally flowing with wine and it was seven o'clock in the evening before the King surrounded by his happy excited people reached the Palace of Whitehall.

'Why could I not be there?' Clive asked himself, but he knew that it would be a mistake for him to go South too soon – in case the Cromwellian supporters in Scotland became vengeful and dangerous.

By this time he had put his estate into good order and was certain that it could not be seized or threatened while he was away.

Clive had no intention of riding the long distance to London or of driving by coach or carriage.

And it was only a few months later that he decided to attend the Palace of Whitehall, as he was determined to see King Charles who he had known well when they were boys together.

If possible he would serve his Majesty in the same way he had attempted to serve him by fighting against his enemies.

Now at last he could afford to travel to the South in a degree of comfort.

So he hired a ship to take him to the Thames.

He travelled with his valet and several others of his extensive staff, including his secretary and butler, to make certain he was comfortable.

Clive could not help but think that he was making up for his very long and dangerous journey home from the Battle of Worcester and the many disreputable miserable places he had been forced to sleep in night after night.

When he did arrive at the Palace of Whitehall, the King was delighted to see him again after so long, and the two of them had so much to relate to each other of all their vicissitudes in the years since they had last met.

King Charles, Clive found, was extremely short of money, as indeed he had been for most of his life.

This was not surprising considering he had so much to restore on his return including his thoroughbred horses, stables, falconers and cormorant keepers.

These, of course, were required for his amusement, but most importantly he was obliged to restore the entire paraphernalia of the Royal Household.

Everything had fallen into desuetude during the last twenty years and the King now began to fully realise that the Restoration was indeed a heroic challenge.

His father, King Charles I, had assembled a great art collection, all of which had been tragically sold after his death by the Officials of the Commonwealth.

King Charles was determined that this should be replaced. He had already acquired some paintings while he was in the Netherlands and he was very excited at the task of starting a new Royal collection.

As soon as he arrived, the Marquis of Morelanton – Clive could now safely and openly use his title – was as enthusiastic as the King was.

The Dutch Government had presented King Charles with a fine collection of twenty-seven Master paintings that included a famous Titian.

The two men looked at the Titian almost with awe – nothing quite so marvellous could have been owned by anyone during the long miserable years of the Cromwellian rule.

The Royal Apartments also needed a great deal of redecoration and refurbishment.

One thousand pounds had already been spent on furniture, but the King's bedroom needed a great deal more spent on it before it was restored to the splendour of the past.

Clive had teased him when they were boys, because Charles had always loved watches and clocks.

There were seven clocks in His Majesty's bedroom and his attendants were continually complaining about the noise they made.

But the question arose daily of how everything was to be paid for.

A few months after his return to England, the King had grumbled ruefully of his position.

He complained to those who questioned him about his expenditure,

"I must tell you that I am not richer. In fact I have not as much money in my purse as when I came to you."

When they were alone the King confided in Clive,

"It is quite obvious to me that that the only solution to my problem is to marry a Queen who will bring me a large dowry!"

Clive made a grimace.

"I have always hated the whole idea of an arranged marriage, Sire, but I suppose as King you will have to put up with it."

"It is certainly not my idea by choice," replied the King. "But things are growing serious and I will have to do something drastic to meet the endless bills that pour in day after day."

The continual lack of money in the Royal coffers was an issue that was regularly deplored not only by the King – it was talked about by almost every member of the Court.

"We will have to find him a bride," one of the most influential of his Courtiers divulged to Clive. "And the first question is what her dowry will be, even before we look to see if she is pretty enough to attract his Majesty!"

Finally Clive was informed that the odds were on the well-endowed Portuguese Infanta, but it was somewhat embarrassing that the King's financial difficulties made the dowry the most important subject to be discussed by the representatives of both countries.

At the same time the King's many extravagances and financial mismanagement were criticised outside the Palace.

The sums of money the King was originally voted by Parliament, which at the time had seemed completely adequate, proved very difficult to collect from a reluctant Treasury.

The King and Clive, because they had known each other for so long, talked frankly when they were alone and could not be overheard.

Clive often told the King that if he had the money himself, he would help him down to his last penny.

But he had to be extremely careful not to fall into debt as that would mean having to dismiss a great number of the people who worked on his Scottish estate.

"What it really comes down to," the King declared finally, "is that you and I, Clive, need to marry into money.

Whatever the woman looks like, if she shines like a guinea, we will be forced to be content with her!"

He sighed before he added,

"I suppose we have to make sacrifices and perhaps the hardest part of all will be to give up a woman we really wish to be with – "

Clive knew without him saying any more what he was thinking.

When he was married, it would not be easy for him to enjoy the company and favours of Barbara Castlemaine.

Clive had met the lady in question just as soon as he had arrived at the Palace of Whitehall.

She was extremely pretty and gave the appearance of always laughing.

A first cousin of the Duke of Buckingham, she had married a Catholic Royalist called Roger Palmer and had succeeded poor Lucy Walter who had died in Paris before the King left for England.

There was no doubt, Clive mused, that Barbara was not only attractive but had definitely captivated the King's heart.

He was at his very best when he was with her and he spent as much time in her company as he could.

She certainly had a special hold over him which no one else had ever contrived to achieve – no one could coax him into a good humour better than Barbara.

She had been married when she was eighteen and her husband was a sensitive and somewhat gloomy man, and this was not really surprising in view of the outrageous behaviour of his wife.

Yet the King reimbursed him by making him the Earl of Castlemaine in the autumn of 1661.

When Clive first arrived at the Palace of Whitehall, he learnt that Barbara had been accorded her own special Apartments there. Her accommodation included nurseries, which would soon prove very necessary.

*

The difficult question of the King's marriage was finally settled.

It was to be with the Portuguese Infanta, Catharine of Braganza.

"You must come with me to my wedding," King Charles implored Clive.

The two men set off together to Portsmouth with a large contingent of the Royal Household.

The Portuguese Ambassador had laid stress on the Queen's dowry and the English were almost mesmerised by the enormous fortune she offered on her marriage.

Dangled before the eyes of the English people, it was fantastic – two million crowns or about three hundred and eighty thousand pounds in those days.

Also the King gained Tangier on the Mediterranean coast of Africa and Bombay on the West coast of India – he had to be shown where the latter was on the map in his study.

What was more important at the time was that the dowry was to be paid in sugar, Brazillian wood and cash.

Lord Clarendon, who had accompanied Charles in exile in France and was now Lord Chancellor, swore to the Portuguese Ambassador that the principal inducement to the Royal marriage was the piety, virtue and comeliness of the Infanta.

Then he gave the game away by asking for Tangier to be handed over quickly to reassure the English!

The courtship had been carried out on the King's behalf in Portugal by the English Ambassador, Sir Richard Fanshawe.

Charles himself wrote flowery letters to the young lady and also to her father and mother.

He even made an effort to write them in Spanish, although he had to ask Lord Clarendon to check his letters over and again for mistakes.

The King and Clarendon were eventually able to inform the English Parliament that the negotiations were complete.

Charles then signed his letters to Catharine,

"The very faithful husband of Your Majesty whose hand he kisses."

Catharine had actually been designated a 'Queen of England', while she was still in Lisbon and a considerable time elapsed before she made the long journey to her new home.

She was escorted in a war ship named *The Royal Charles*.

When she finally arrived in Portsmouth, one of her first actions was to ask for a cup of tea – this was a surprise as the British national beverage was ale, which was what the Queen was offered instead.

Later on Queen Catharine did a great deal to make the drinking of tea popular and in the years ahead it was to become an English habit.

Although she was on English soil, the country was still worrying over the actual delivery of the dowry and the garrison at Tangier.

But long before her arrival in England a far more difficult problem had arisen which the King and Clive had discussed when they were alone.

Until the Royal wedding actually took place, the Queen could not assume the married state.

But the question was – what sort of wedding?

Queen Catharine was a Roman Catholic like most of the Royal Princesses of Europe and her religion had already caused dissatisfaction among many Englishmen.

Many of them had disapproved of the Portuguese match from the outset and there were whispers and protests against the Mass, friars, confessions and other aspects of the Catholic Church.

The King's marriage was altogether distasteful to Protestant Englishmen.

The Portuguese Ambassador, however, had assured King Charles that his bride would not be at all difficult on the subject and that she was most willing to do anything which would make him happy and his people content.

From the prestigious Office of the Privy Council Lord Clarendon had written some notes to King Charles on the subject.

He told His Majesty that he must have a Catholic wedding ceremony in secret to be followed by a Protestant ceremony in public for the sake of the legitimacy of any children from the marriage.

Queen Catharine, Clarendon assured the King, was prepared to submit to this plan.

The King wrote in reply,

"*I hope she has consulted the Jesuits.*"

"*She will do what is necessary for herself and her children,*" Lord Clarendon responded rather pompously.

In the end it was all comfortably arranged.

A brief and secret Catholic ceremony was held first in the bedroom assigned to Queen Catharine in the official residence of the Governor-General of Portsmouth. Then a

Protestant marriage took place in the Great Chamber of the same building.

His Chapel, it was discovered, was too small for the number of people who had to be accommodated.

The King and his Queen sat on two specially built thrones behind a rail to keep away the spectators.

The Queen wore a rose-coloured gown covered in lovers-knots and blue ribbons and after the ceremony was over these were cut off according to a Portuguese tradition and everyone was given a piece. And the lace of her veil was covered with patriotic emblems of her new country including Tudor roses.

The King presented the Governor's Chapel with an altar cloth embroidered with a view of Lisbon.

They returned poste haste to London the next day where Her Majesty was welcomed with all the pomp due to a Royal Consort.

The procession which carried her from Whitehall to Hampton Court, where the honeymoon was to be spent was the most magnificent ever seen on the Thames.

But already at Hampton Court Barbara Castlemaine the Royal mistress, exercised her power over the King.

As a somewhat petty gesture she refused to light a torch outside her Apartment door as a welcome for the new Queen.

Because of his marriage to the Infanta she managed to make the King feel guilty and therefore he spent more time with Barbara than he should have done.

Later Clive, who was present at all the ceremonies and celebrations, was one of the few people who realised that things did not go as easily as the King had hoped.

The Queen's health did not permit their marriage to be consummated that night and King Charles jokingly said afterwards to his sister that perhaps it was just as well that the long sea journey had upset her.

He himself had suffered from a terrible journey to Portsmouth and in fact as he said to Clive when they were alone,

"Matters could not have gone more stupidly."

It seemed to be a family misfortune because exactly the same had happened on his sister's wedding night.

It was perhaps Clive who worried more over the Queen than his friend the King.

He had discovered that she had been brought up in a Convent in a most restrictive fashion and now that she was twenty-three years old, he was told privately that she was more like an English woman of forty would have been.

Also he was told in a whisper that when the Queen was informed of her intended marriage, she made one of her rare sorties from the Royal Palace in Lisbon to go on a pilgrimage to some Saint's shrine.

She had taken with her a suite of over a hundred retainers – they included numerous confessors, besides a Jewish perfumer and a barber.

Clive repeated all this to the King who laughed and joked,

"She will soon get used to our strange English ways and habits!"

Clive could only hope that he was right.

There was one interest she at least shared with the King that no one had expected.

She was most skilful at archery and having enjoyed a great deal more practice, she was rather better at it than her husband.

The first crisis in Queen Catharine's married life was something she had not expected and it naturally upset her.

When they arrived in London, Barbara Castlemaine was waiting for her.

She had already been informed what had happened at Portsmouth and she was determined to show her power over the King and sacrifice none of it to any other woman.

Barbara was far too clever to meet the King with a gloomy face or to reproach him with her sensuous lips.

She was very sure of her great beauty and she was always referred to as 'the lovely Countess'.

The sight of her smocks and pretty linen petticoats drying in the Royal Privy garden strongly affected the great diarist, Samuel Pepys, and he was to remember the thrill they gave him for the rest of his life.

Maybe it was her indefatigable buoyancy of spirit that made Barbara so special.

In those days women on the whole were quiet and rather withdrawn into themselves, but whatever it might have been, Barbara was great fun for the young gentlemen who enjoyed her company.

She took care to keep a good table for anyone who called on her and her *cuisine* was praised by the French Ambassador, a renowned connoisseur of good food, so it was obviously outstanding.

Barbara was also genuinely kind-hearted.

On one occasion when a small boy was hurt when a scaffold collapsed in the theatre, she was the only Court Lady to go to his assistance.

Now waiting for the Queen in her own extensive Apartments in Whitehall Palace, Barbara lifted up her firm and beautifully curved chin.

She then vowed secretly to herself that she would not surrender her Royal lover to any woman.

There was no need for her to worry that she would

not attract the rapt attention and tenderness of other men as whatever they might feel about the Queen, a great number of them found Barbara irresistible.

Just like every woman she was determined to draw attention to herself by her appearance.

When the King and the Members of his Court dined to celebrate the arrival of the Queen, Barbara Castlemaine outshone all the other ladies present.

Throughout his life King Charles's way of dealing with a woman's tears or hysteria was to present her with something to 'cheer her up' – just as a parent might give a sweetmeat to a child.

Where Queen Catharine was concerned her obvious piety gave him plenty of opportunity to placate her.

The Queen had such a passion for religious relics that she had brought with her great coffers of them. They were all covered in red velvet embroidered with the Royal Arms of England.

King Charles added to her relics with a number of crosses and other pious ornaments.

Barbara Castlemaine had very different ideas and was far more difficult to appease.

She raged at the King, demanding that he should make her Lady of the Bedchamber to the new Queen and eventually, worn out by the endless arguments, he agreed.

He explained lamely he had ruined her reputation which had been 'untainted' until Barbara became 'friends' with him.

It was an extraordinary way to behave and at the same time a considerable insult to his wife.

Queen Catharine however had already learnt a great deal about the King without his being aware of it.

She recognised Barbara's name on the list of Ladies of the Bedchamber presented to her for her agreement and crossed it out angrily.

However, when Barbara was first presented to her, to everyone's surprise she greeted her cordially, but it was her poor understanding of English that had prevented her from realising who Barbara really was.

The moment she discovered the truth, the Queen's eyes filled with tears, her nose started to bleed profusely and she collapsed on the floor in hysterics.

The King, when he was told of what had happened, sent Lord Clarendon to reason with her but needless to say his Lordship failed completely.

The King was faced with torrents of tears and the Queen's threat that she would return to Portugal.

The King's sister was extremely shocked by her brother's behaviour and wrote to him,

"It is sad to hear she has grieved beyond measure, and to speak frankly I think it is with reason."

However the King merely played more tennis with his friend Clive and swam most mornings in the Thames.

It took Queen Catharine some time to discover that hysterics and threats were quite ineffective where Charles was concerned.

Catharine found out that the strength she required to deal with him was the goodness of her character and the sweetness of her nature.

Clive, in an effort to help the King, talked to her gently.

He told her that her dignity, her tact and restraint were far more effective than rudeness and tantrums would ever be and he certainly helped to calm down the storm.

She therefore behaved as Clive begged her to do as Queen of England.

Whilst Barbara foolishly became more noisy and as quite a number of people felt, more vulgar.

*

While all this turmoil was going on, Clive himself was being bombarded, although that was not the word she would have used, by the Countess of Dalwaynnie.

She had made up her mind as soon as she saw him.

She thought he was undoubtedly one of the most handsome young gentlemen she had ever seen.

And he would surely be just the right husband she desired for Nancy.

As soon as she and Nancy had arrived in London, the Countess started to nose around the Palace searching for the perfect husband for her beloved daughter.

She was determined Nancy should have the highest possible title, but the majority of the King's Courtiers were already married and were anyway too old.

Those who were not made it clear to the Countess from the moment of their acquaintance that they were not interested in young girls.

Then when Clive arrived her spirits rose.

As Marchioness of Morelanton, Nancy would have exactly the position in the social world she craved for her.

The Countess soon became well aware of potential danger from the beautiful Alissia.

She had tried to make it clear to her husband that one unmarried daughter at Court was enough, but Bruce had been determined to bring his beloved Alissia with him.

And she came with him for the Coronation and he knew that it would have broken Alissia's heart not to see the pomp and glory of the great day – beside the fact that she had always had a most respectful admiration for the King.

Clive had written to her father regularly during the years they were apart.

Alissia had leapt for joy when she heard that he was coming from Scotland to London to join the King.

Clive wrote in a letter to Bruce,

"*We have certainly waited long for this marvellous moment and the King is entitled to all the applause and adulation he can get considering the way he has suffered for such a long time.*"

"And Clive has suffered too," Bruce added when he read the letter out to Alissia. "He returned home to find his brother had been killed by the Roundheads and his father was in ill health."

He paused before he added,

"He has written to me over the years telling me how much he has improved his estate and made the Castle more habitable than before. I have a great admiration for that young man and I look forward to seeing him again."

"And I very much look forward to seeing him too," said Alissia. "You remember Nanny gave him two pieces of my hair and he told me it had brought him luck."

"Of course it did, and as Nanny is coming with us to London, I am sure Clive will want to see her too."

They had set off, travelling in the most comfortable way they could, not only with Nanny but also with Jimbo, Alissia's spaniel.

"I cannot leave Jimbo behind, Papa," she insisted, as she knew how much the Countess disliked dogs. "And I will do my best to keep him quiet and out of sight."

"Of course," her father agreed at once. "I am sure he would pine away without you. I only wish I could take all my horses too!"

"We must not stay in London for ever, Papa."

"Perhaps it will have to be for a long time," he had replied. "In which case we will send for the horses and anything else you may require."

She smiled at him.

He thought that there would be no other woman at Court – not even the famous Barbara Castlemaine of whom he had heard a great deal – to equal Alissia.

She had certainly grown very lovely as the years had passed.

Her fair hair, which was now arranged on the top of her head, caught the gold of the sun and glittered as she moved.

Her perfect pink and white skin was an ideal setting for her deep blue eyes, which her father had sometimes described as 'a stormy sea'.

"I don't mind your saying that about the colour of my eyes," Alissia laughed. "But I would hate you to think that *I* was stormy!"

"You are never that, my darling. I'm afraid that so many men will find you irresistible when we reach London that I will see very little of you."

What he had not expected was that the Countess would have set her heart on capturing Clive as her future son-in-law.

She was completely determined that he should not be attracted by her stepdaughter and she was too clever not to realise that while her daughter was good-looking, Alissia was undoubtedly a great beauty.

She had managed by becoming friendly with the King's Administrators to ensure that she and Nancy were invited to the small private parties that often took place in the evening at the Royal Palace.

The Countess kept these secret from her husband and Alissia.

"We are just going to have dinner tonight with a friend on the other side of the Royal Palace," she would say. "I've ordered you both a delicious dinner and I don't expect we will be very late."

It never struck Bruce for a moment that his wife was being deceitful.

He himself had been received with delight and the King had made it very clear how welcome he was at Court.

It did, however, strike him as a little strange that he was seldom asked to dine with the King, and Alissia was never invited.

It seemed a little odd too that Clive, when he met him, had not asked to see Alissia.

He was to find out later it was because he had been informed by the Countess that she had been left behind in the country.

There was so much to see and so many activities she had never encountered before in her life to attract her attention.

Thus for the first two weeks after Alissia arrived in London she had no idea that Clive, now the Marquis of Morelanton, was also living in an Apartment at the Royal Palace of Whitehall.

CHAPTER FOUR

Bruce was invited by the King to go to Hampton Court Palace to meet the Queen.

Of course he was delighted to accept.

It meant that the Countess had to be invited as well to the exclusion of a disappointed and resentful Lady-in-Waiting.

Alissia, naturally, was left behind.

As Nancy was busy with her new friends, she was alone in their Apartment, which she much preferred.

She had her delightful spaniel, Jimbo, with her who she adored and he adored her.

She talked to him and found him, she thought, more intelligent than most of the people she had to talk to.

One day she saw the keeper who looked after the King's dogs from her bedroom window.

He was taking the dogs out from their kennels and she ran down to join him.

For a long time she had wanted to look at the dogs close to and pat them, but she knew it would be very wrong of her to do so when the King was in residence.

Now with the King away from London, there was just a nice man who smiled at her as she joined him.

"I see you 'as a dog too, my Lady," he remarked.

"He is so longing to meet the dogs you are looking after," replied Alissia. "He is very lonely having no one to talk to except for me!"

"I can't see that'll be an imposition," the man said gallantly.

He was older than Alissia thought and he told her that he had been looking after dogs ever since he was a small boy and that his name was Bill.

"I be much more fond of 'em than I be of 'orses," Bill rambled on. "Me brothers all goes to the stables, but I wants to stay with the dogs."

"I can see that you love them, Bill."

They talked for some time and then, when he took the dogs for a walk in the Park behind the Palace, she went with him.

Jimbo obviously thought it was the best thing that had ever happened.

He played with the King's spaniels, avoiding the older ones who might think of him as an intruder.

"I think His Majesty is lucky to have such very fine animals," Alissia commented.

"He chooses everyone of 'em himself," replied Bill, "and he calls 'em all by their right names. He likes to 'ave two or perhaps three in 'is rooms with 'im every day. He chooses which shall 'ave the honour after they've been for a walk."

Alissia laughed.

She thought it was an amusing idea and something her father ought to do and she would tell him about it when he came back from Hampton Court.

She had something else to tell him and she had not had a chance before he left because he had been so busy.

It was that she did not like the man she felt that her stepmother was pressing on her.

His name was Lord Pronett.

He had noticed her in the gardens of the Palace and introduced himself to her stepmother.

The Countess obviously thought him charming and she encouraged him to call on them in the mornings when they were in the gardens as well as in the early evenings when her father was attending Court.

Alissia did not know exactly why, but she disliked Lord Pronett as soon as she met him.

Every time he touched her hand it somehow made her shudder.

Lord Pronett was in fact a very extraordinary man.

He had been intelligent enough against all the odds to worm his way into the Palace.

He was born plain Frederick Brown, the son of a schoolmaster in a small village in Norfolk.

As the school had very few pupils, the master was poorly paid and he often had a great deal of time on his hands, so he had plenty of time to educate his son far more thoroughly than the other local boys and girls.

Freddie, as he was always called, grew up knowing a great deal about subjects that never entered the heads of the villagers and it gave him a strong ambition to better himself.

When he was seventeen years old, his father died unexpectedly and his mother told him that he had to earn his own living in the world outside their small village.

On an impulse he went to the big house which was some way from the village, where he had not been before and offered himself as secretary to the owner.

This was Lord Pronett, an old man who lived alone in the house of his ancestors.

He was very lonely as he had never married and had no surviving relations. At least if there were any, they did not bother about him and he seldom had a visitor, but at the same time he lived in reasonable comfort.

His only major difficulty was that his servants were continually leaving him. They found the house too isolated and the village, which was over two miles away, had little to offer them.

Freddie proved himself to be a most efficient and useful secretary to Lord Pronett and the old man was really delighted with him.

He found that Lord Pronett was far richer than he had thought he was and Freddie persuaded his Lordship to spend some money on new horses which he enjoyed riding.

He was well fed in the house and looked after by the servants and treated as their superior.

He much enjoyed being with Lord Pronett and had no intention of leaving him.

Because the house was so isolated and he seldom appeared in public, Lord Pronett was completely ignored by the Cromwellians.

His Lordship and Freddie therefore learnt only from the newspapers what was happening in other parts of the country and as his Lordship's eyesight was failing, Freddie would read the newspapers aloud to him.

He soon learnt, however, that Lord Pronett was not really interested in political matters in the country and so he merely read him the reports of race meetings and other sporting items, while keeping the main news for himself.

The years passed by.

Freddie was thrilled when Oliver Cromwell died and he knew it was the end of all the dismal accounts of battles won by the Cromwellians and the reports of those who suffered the death penalty after every uprising.

Freddie was so elated at the news that he ran in to Lord Pronett's bedroom and told him excitedly what had happened.

It was only to find that his Lordship had completely forgotten who Oliver Cromwell was and was therefore not in the least interested in what he had to say.

His Lordship's memory had been failing for some time, but Freddie thought he was much worse now than he had ever been.

If it took a long time for King Charles to claim the Throne of England, it took nearly as long for Lord Pronett to die.

When he eventually did so, Freddie realised, as he should have done before, that there were no relations or friends to notify.

He was the only mourner in the village Church as Lord Pronett was interred in the tomb of his ancestors.

When Freddie went back to the big house, he was aware it was virtually empty of servants – they had been leaving one by one when Lord Pronett lay bedridden.

Now the last couple, who had been at the big house longer than the others, were leaving for the North.

"We've 'eard of a place that will just suit us fine," the man had said, "and at least we'll see some friendly faces and not feel isolated as we've been in this 'ole."

"I am sorry you must leave," countered Freddie.

"Well you take my advice," the woman said, "a fine upstanding young man like you should be findin' yourself a pretty wife and somewhere where there's a bit of fun and frolic."

"I am sure you are right," smiled Freddie.

As he waved them goodbye he realised he was now alone in the house.

As Lord Pronett's trusted secretary he had the key to his Lordship's will locked away in the safe.

When he took the will out, he found that the house and grounds were left to a distant cousin, but Freddie knew that he had been killed fighting against the Cromwellians in some obscure battle in the North.

There were various sums of money bequeathed to people who were already dead or of whom he had never heard.

Then as he looked down at his Lordship's signature a sudden idea came to him. At first it was so stupendous that he almost laughed at it as madness.

Then slowly, as if his brain was gradually accepting the thought and turning it from fantasy to fact, he realised what he should do.

He lay awake most of that night thinking it all out in detail.

Finally on the following morning he was aware that everything had fallen into place just like a jigsaw puzzle.

Lord Pronett was now dead and there was no one to mourn him.

He would be extremely stupid, which he was not, if he did not recognise the possibilities for himself.

First of all he would change the will, naming his son Frederick Pronett as sole legatee.

This was easy for him to do, as the will had been made nearly twenty years earlier and there was no one to even remember its existence.

Secondly Lord Pronett had died ostensibly without an heir to his title.

'But who is to know? Who can possibly say that Lord Pronett was not married twenty-nine years ago and I was born the following year?' Freddie asked himself.

There was no one around to know.

If questions were asked in the village, it would be pretty easy to convince them that Lord Pronett had treated him like a son, but had kept his identity a secret.

This was because he had married a wife who was well-known to be a Royalist – Lord Pronett was therefore frightened that his son might become another victim of the Cromwellians.

Freddie thought it all out very carefully as if it was a story someone was telling him.

He then decided that his mother's family had been well respected and had always been accepted at the Royal Palace.

She had been engaged, he also decided, to someone of rank in Court circles, but she had then fallen in love with Lord Pronett when he was still a young man and had not yet succeeded to the title. They had run away and married on the eve of her wedding day.

They had hidden themselves in the country, moving from place to place, until finally old Lord Pronett, living in the family house, died.

His son inherited his title together with everything else he possessed.

For a long time because they were frightened of the Cromwellians, he, Freddie, had been hidden away by his mother's friends.

When they too passed on to a better world and he was forced, because he had nowhere else to go, to come to live with his father.

To his neighbours in Norfolk Lord Pronett had been a lonely unmarried man with apparently few acquaintances to keep him company.

Freddie had then become his father's secretary and had of course been believed.

As he turned the whole plot over and over in his mind, Freddie thought it was a foolproof story.

After all there was no one in the least interested who could find fault with it or claim the title.

So he took over the house and estate and only let the Vicar into the secret that he was in fact the old man's son.

The Vicar who was new to the district was most impressed and he had agreed with Freddie that he would be wise to keep his real name secret.

He must continue to remain as Freddie Brown until the Stuarts returned to their rightful place.

Because he was lonely, although he was now rich, Freddie felt the past years had taken a long time to pass.

Yet he was too wise to make any move until King Charles had been crowned and he then knew that his story would now reach a new chapter.

Now at last he could do what he had always wanted to do, he could go to London as Lord Pronett and ingratiate himself with the King.

Because he was intelligent he had read everything he could about the Stuarts and their predecessors.

He had also learnt by reading the newspapers that King Charles II was very depressed at finding his father's art collection had been sold.

This Freddie recognised at once was his dream-card that would move him into the Royal circles quicker than anything else.

He must, however, wait until the Coronation had actually taken place.

He found the months passed incredibly slowly and his impatience grew day by day until he could finally set out for London.

He had prepared everything ready for the moment he could leave – his clothes, his wide knowledge of Court protocol and, most importantly of all, two pictures that he was taking to the King as a gift.

Finally he arrived at the Palace of Whitehall.

When he told the Lord Chamberlain who he was and what he had brought for King Charles, he was taken into the Royal presence almost immediately.

It took four footmen following behind him to carry the Van Dyck and the Holbein masterpieces he had taken off the walls of Pronett Hall.

They were, he knew, the very best of the real Lord Pronett's collection.

The King was naturally delighted with them and he took Freddie to see the gallery where the pictures he had already collected were hanging.

Freddie had taken a great deal of trouble in learning all about the great artists and he found that he knew even more about art than the King himself.

They had a most interesting and learned discussion.

"I am exceedingly grateful to you for your gifts," said the King, "and you must tell me where you are living, Lord Pronett."

Freddie made an expressive gesture with his hands.

"I have been living in the country ever since I was a small boy, Sire, simply because my father had a title and our family had always been supporters of the Stuarts. He was always a likely victim of the Cromwellians."

"Of course you must have been too, Lord Pronett, and it was stupid of me to ask the question. I am sure your family is a very ancient one."

"Very ancient indeed, Sire, but I am afraid there are not many of us left."

The King smiled.

"Then it is obvious that is something you will have to put right. As I have to marry, you will have to think of it too and it should be quite simple for you to find a really suitable bride here in London."

He offered Lord Pronett a room at the Royal Palace while he searched for a house or a flat in the City.

*

And so it was hardly surprising that he soon met the Countess of Dalwaynnie.

She learnt from the Gentlemen-in-Waiting who he was and that he was extremely well off with a large estate in Norfolk.

The Countess had already made up her mind that Nancy should marry Clive, the Marquis of Morelanton.

She was well aware that Bruce had hidden him after the Battle of Worcester and that it was Alissia's locks of hair that had been so instrumental in saving his life.

So she was determined that Clive should not meet Alissia until he was irrevocably engaged to Nancy.

The Countess herself was extremely crafty when she wanted her own way and she managed to manoeuvre Clive into dancing with Nancy more than once at every party.

Even when, shortly before the Coronation, Alissia came to London with her father, the Countess told Clive that she was still in the country and she then contrived to entertain him in their Apartment when Alissia had gone out with her father – perhaps down the river or to see the sights of London which he was only too eager to show her.

All the more she liked her idea that if Lord Pronett married Alissia, he would take her away to the house he was always talking about in Norfolk.

And that would definitely leave the way clear for Nancy to marry Clive.

She had already played on his feelings by telling him how fond her husband was of him.

And it was obvious that Clive must reply that he was alive only because of the cleverness of Nanny and also thanks to the horse Bruce had given him, which had carried him safely away to Scotland.

"Of course you want to show him how grateful you are," said the Countess, "and, as he is so fond of you, I can think of no better way than that you should become one of the family."

She had made this very clear as soon as they had met while Alissia and her father were still in the country.

The King, because he was very fond of him, was determined if he had to be married Clive should be married too.

"Have a good look around, Clive," he suggested, "and see which of the women, and Heaven knows there are enough of them, is likely to be more complacent and easier to manage than the others."

Clive knew quite well what the King meant by that comment.

The Queen naturally had made a huge scene about Barbara Castlemaine being at Hampton Court.

There was little doubt that Barbara always looked exquisitely lovely.

Her dark hair with its auburn glints would shake a little when she laughed and it seemed to catch the sunshine and she was more elaborately dressed than any of the other women who were there to attend on Her Majesty.

She might have been a little apprehensive about the position she found herself in, but she gave the strongest impression of being absolutely sure of herself.

It struck Clive, as it had so many other people, that Roger Palmer, now the Earl of Castlemaine, was a pathetic figure in many ways.

He was powerless to control his wife and he had undoubtedly raged against her in private, yet was obliged publicly to accept the title she had earned by her infidelity with the King.

Watching them at Hampton Court, Clive saw him elegantly dressed and wearing a curled periwig, which was not particularly becoming to his pale and somewhat insipid face.

There was no doubt that his wife saw him approach, but she did not acknowledge him until he was beside her.

Then she glanced round and gave a start of surprise and made him a rather mocking curtsy, which he returned with a courteous bow.

As he turned away without speaking, Clive knew that he bored her and she irritated him.

'That is what I myself might be doing,' he reflected with utmost horror, 'if I stay at Court and marry the wrong girl.'

In point of fact because he had been so besieged by his relations, he had been thinking seriously of marriage.

He did not envy the King marrying a woman he had never even seen, however attractive the reports might have been about her.

He told himself he had no intention of marrying anyone like Barbara Castlemaine, who would be so openly unfaithful to him.

Even as he was ruminating about himself, he was aware that the Countess of Dalwaynnie was near him.

"I am so glad you are here," she simpered. "I want you to be kind to my little Nancy when the Court returns to

Whitehall. She is feeling rather left out since only a few girls of her own age have had the privilege of meeting the new Queen."

Clive was silent for a moment.

He realised only too well what would happen if he appeared interested in Nancy.

If he spent any of his time with her, he would put himself in a hopeless position and the older ladies of the Court would say he had made his intentions obvious.

He would therefore be obliged, whether he wanted to or not, to offer her marriage.

Equally he could never forget for a moment how much he owed Bruce.

Then to his relief there was a sudden surge towards the door, as obviously either the King or the Queen was approaching.

"Please do forgive me," he murmured hastily to the Countess, bowed and hurried away.

*

When the Court moved in dramatic style down the river back to Whitehall, the Countess made up her mind that Clive should become engaged to Nancy as quickly as possible.

As they all arrived at the door of their Apartment, Alissia ran to greet her father.

As she did so, the Countess could not help noticing how lovely and elegant she looked.

And this convinced her that she must be removed as quickly as possible from the Palace.

At first she thought she might send Alissia back to Worcestershire and then she realised that Bruce would not agree as he loved having his daughter with him in London.

Later the Countess met Lord Pronett again and she found him sitting next to her at a party given immediately after the Court's return to Whitehall.

She sensed again even more urgently that here was the lifeline she needed.

There was indeed something about him that made him seem a little different from the other gentlemen at the table, but that did not worry her.

"I am very anxious, Lord Pronett," she began, "for you to help me with my stepdaughter. She is not in the least happy because she is suddenly being pursued by a most unpleasant fellow of whom we all disapprove."

She gave a deep sigh before she continued,

"I am frightened, really frightened, that he may hurt her in some way. Will you come and meet her tomorrow morning when she takes her dog for a walk in St. James's Park?"

"I would be delighted to do so," replied Freddie.

It was important for him to become intimate with people who were close to the King and there was no doubt that the King was particularly friendly and respectful to the Earl of Dalwaynnie.

*

The following morning Alissia went outside for her usual walk with Jimbo.

To her surprise her stepmother, who was normally up late, was already there and talking to the man she had met before and disliked.

"Oh, there you are, Alissia," the Countess smiled. "You know Lord Pronett, of course. He is particularly keen on dogs and tells me that he wants to buy one like Jimbo."

This was something new to Freddie, but he did not deny it.

"I feel sure," replied Alissia, "that Lord Pronett will be more interested in the King's dogs, which should be appearing at any moment."

Even as she spoke there was a sound of barking as the King's spaniels emerged from their kennels and were passing on their way to the Park.

Alissia waved to her friend, Bill.

As he watched her, Freddie felt that she was the most attractive and beautiful girl he had ever seen.

If he could marry someone like her, he thought, she would certainly grace his house in the country – and she and her aristocratic family would make it possible for him to be regularly in attendance at the Royal Palace.

He had made up his mind the moment he arrived that this was the world he wished to live in and this was indeed possible as he had claimed to be a loyal Royalist throughout the Cromwellian times.

And everybody believed him to be the genuine Peer he claimed to be.

He was quite prepared to marry anyone to further his ambitions, but he could never have imagined he would be more or less offered anyone so lovely or so ethereal as Alissia.

She was now patting the King's dogs with the sun shining on her golden hair and the dogs seemed to greet her as enthusiastically as she greeted them.

Watching Lord Pronett, the Countess knew that she had scored a victory.

She quickly drew him away to talk to him privately.

Now it would not be difficult to put into operation her scheme for Nancy.

She had been worried ever since she had arrived at the Palace that Clive would see Alissia and if he did so, he would undoubtedly be only too willing to repay his debt to her husband by asking Alissia to be his wife.

It was all, she told herself, a question of timing and that meant that the quicker Alissia was out of the way the better.

"I am so concerned about her," she cooed in a soft voice to Freddie. "This man pursuing her is completely relentless. Although my husband does not listen to me, I am really afraid, because, although you may well feel that I am being hysterical, I think he might kidnap her."

"*Kidnap her!*" exclaimed Freddie.

"When a man becomes infatuated by a woman he will do anything to get his own way and, although I will do my best, I cannot protect Alissia all the time."

"No, of course not," he answered vaguely.

When the keeper passed on into the Park, Alissia began to walk slowly and rather reluctantly back towards where she thought her stepmother might be.

It was then, before the dogs were out of sight, that the King, accompanied by Clive, came out of another door with tennis rackets in their hands.

Alissia stopped still.

She was right in the path of the two men.

Only as they reached her, did she remember to drop a deep curtsy.

Even as she did so, Clive exclaimed,

"*Alissia!* You must be Alissia! It is *you.* I have been hunting for you everywhere and had been told you were in the country!"

"No, I came here with Papa over two months ago," Alissia replied. "I was so hoping that I would see you – "

"And I wanted to see you too – "

"Now what is all this!" asked the King. "And why, Alissia, have you been hiding yourself? I have asked your stepmother where you were and she has told me you were in Worcestershire."

"I came to London when my Papa came, Sire," she repeated.

"Then you have been hiding yourself from me," the King said, "and I am most upset that you did not come to Hampton Court."

"I was really longing to come, Sire, but I was not invited. Please do not be angry with Stepmama. It would upset Papa."

"Which of course we must never do," laughed the King.

He glanced at Clive as he spoke and realised that while he was talking, he had been gazing at Alissia.

There was an expression in his eyes that the King had not seen before.

"I believe, Clive, that this is the young lady whose hair saved your life," he remarked.

"That is indeed true, Sire, and I have been looking for her ever since."

"I am not at all surprised," muttered the King. "I intend to invite you, Lady Alissia, to come and dine with us soon. Actually it is a command, so you cannot refuse!"

"Your Majesty is very gracious and I would love to dine with you. It is an honour I have been hoping for ever since I arrived in London."

"And Clive had just said that he has been looking for you. But now I must take him away because we are about to play a game of tennis."

The King turned away as he spoke, but Clive turned back to ask Alissia,

"Why have you kept away from me? I had no idea that you were here in London all this time."

"Do you really still have my two pieces of hair?" she then asked him coyly.

"Of course I have, Alissia, and I intend to show you them at the first opportunity!"

He smiled at her in a way that made her remember how he had kissed her all those years ago.

Then with an obvious effort he ran after the King, who by this time had reached the gate that led to the tennis court.

'I have found him! I have found him at last!' she thought to herself excitedly.

Forgetting about her stepmother and Lord Pronett who were not in sight, she ran back into the Royal Palace and up the stairs that led to their own Apartment.

Nanny was there looking much older, but she was still as neat and tidy as she had been all the years she had spent in service.

"What do you think, Nanny!" cried Alissia. "I have just seen Clive More – I mean the Marquis of Morelanton! I hoped he was somewhere in the Palace, but although I have looked and looked it is only now I have seen him. He looks very much the same as when he came to our nursery and you hid him in your bed."

"I've been prayin' ever so hard that he'd find you sooner or later, dearie, but her Ladyship made me promise her on the Bible that I'd not tell you he was in the Royal Palace of Whitehall."

Alissia looked at Nanny in sheer surprise.

"Why should she do that?"

"Your guess is as good as mine, dearie. You knows the answer without me tellin' you."

Alissia stared at her.

Then as if Nanny had spoken aloud, she said,

"You mean Stepmama wants him to marry Nancy?"

"That's what she wants, and that's what she's been plannin'. It's only because I wouldn't break my word that I didn't tell you days ago what she were after."

Alissia drew in her breath.

"I never imagined she would feel like that."

Then she murmured almost to herself,

"At least I have found him now – "

At the same time she was afraid it might be too late.

Later that day her father returned from a meeting he had been summoned to attend at the Royal Palace.

Alissia contrived to be alone with him.

"Why did you not tell me, Papa," she asked, "that Clive More, whom we have talked about so often and is now the Marquis of Morelanton, is here in the Palace."

"I wanted to tell you, my darling Alissia, but your stepmother was so insistent that you were still too young to attend the more formal parties at the Royal Palace."

"Nancy only yesterday let the cat out of the bag, without meaning to, that when she and Stepmama went out in the evening and told us that they were going to friends, they really attended small intimate parties organised by the King at which there was dancing!"

His lips tightened.

He knew it was a mistake to make trouble between his wife and his daughter.

But he was only too well aware that because Alissia was much more beautiful than Nancy, his wife was jealous of her and tried to put her down in his estimation whenever she could.

But he was too wise to argue.

He just let her talk and talk and then ignored what she had said to him.

He was sure that as they had now met again that Clive would find Alissia as attractive and as beautiful as he did himself.

He dismissed the idea of Clive marrying Nancy as he had thought, when it was very obviously suggested by his wife, that she was reaching far too high and asking too much for her daughter.

Equally he had no intention of restricting Alissia in any way.

Only now did he understand how he had been made a fool of and it annoyed him.

Yet if possible he did not want to quarrel with his wife as she always became hysterical.

If it ended in tears, he always had to apologise and say it was all his fault.

Now he realised that he should have made certain as soon as they arrived that Alissia was not shut out of any of the festivities that she could be invited to.

He had been foolish in believing his wife when she had told him that they were just dining with or meeting up with friends.

But she *was* his wife and he had no intention, if he could help it, of fighting over the two girls.

Nanny on the other hand had a great deal more to say to Alissia.

"If you asks me," she had pontificated, "a man of the Marquis's age should choose his own wife and not let them other women pick one for him."

"Perhaps he really does want to marry Nancy – "

"I don't believe it," retorted Nanny. "It was you he were asking for and I heard her mother say not once but several times, 'Oh, Alissia's quite happy in the country, and anyway it's only possible for us to bring one girl to the Court at a time'."

She slapped her bundle noisily down on the table and went on,

"If his Lordship believes that, then he'll certainly believe anythin'. If you asks me he'll be really angry at bein' bamboozled."

"I do hope not," said Alissia, "because that would upset Papa. But I would love to see Clive again and I am longing to find out if he still has the two locks you cut off my hair."

She gave a sigh of satisfaction and added,

"They certainly brought him luck!"

"That be true," answered Nanny. "I've found out that now he's the Marquis of Morelanton after his father's death, he has a vast Castle over the border in Scotland, and a very fine house, if he wishes to use it, in London."

"I hope I will be able to see it, Nanny. I expect you would like to see it too. You have often talked about the London houses you worked in before you came to us. You told me they had large nurseries on the very top floor."

"That be true enough, dearie. In them days children had to be seen and not heard."

Alissia laughed.

"I expect it's the same today. Pushed away at the top of the house, so that no one can hear them cry!"

Nanny's eyes softened.

"Your mother always wanted you with her, dearie, and a lovelier lady never walked this earth."

"I so often think about her, Nanny, and I know just how happy she made Papa. Although I do know that he is very fond of Stepmama, she certainly does not mean the same to him as Mama did."

"No, of course not, dearie. You mark my words, if two people really love each other and that be true enough of your father and mother, there's no one else who can ever take their place."

"That is what I have always thought, Nanny, and if I ever do marry, I want a man who loves me and who never looks at anyone else."

She was thinking how much the poor Queen must resent Barbara Castlemaine in the entourage at Hampton Court, and that she was now firmly established in a large number of grand rooms in the Royal Palace.

"I just know what you're thinkin'," said Nanny. "If I was the Queen, I'd go straight back to where I'd come from and tell His Majesty he can keep his 'fancy' women, but not under the same roof as me!"

Alissia laughed.

Then she put her finger to her lips.

"Be careful, Nanny. If you talk like that we will all be sent back to the country in disgrace. Everyone knows that the King adores Barbara Castlemaine and she really is extremely beautiful."

"Beauty is as beauty does," grumbled Nancy. "If you asks me, it ain't at all respectable and it's not the way a decent woman behaves."

Alissia knew it was no use arguing – Nanny had her principles and she actually agreed with them.

Equally Barbara Castlemaine had to be accepted by everyone who waited on the King from the lowest in the scullery up to the highest Peer.

Yet she had no particular desire to think about it at this moment.

It was so exciting to have found Clive – or rather the Marquis, as he now was.

It was very difficult to think of him except as Clive More, as she had for the past nine years.

Alissia felt that they had so much to talk about and so much to remember and she could only hope that when he came back from playing tennis with the King, he would somehow contrive to see her again.

'I do wish I could go and watch them,' she thought wistfully.

Then she knew it would look as if she was running after Clive and he might be embarrassed by her.

At the same time she felt that her father would help her to see Clive and talk to him as she longed to do.

She opened the door of the room that Nanny called 'the nursery' because it was in here that she washed and ironed Alissia's clothes.

As she did so, she heard one of the servants saying,

"This way, my Lord."

Peeping discreetly over the banisters she saw Lord Pronett walking into the drawing room.

Without his hat his hair looked very dark and rather greasy and she watched his head until it was out of sight.

Then she felt a little shiver go through her.

Alissia did not know why, but there was something about him that she believed was definitely wrong.

Yet she could not put it into words.

CHAPTER FIVE

Alissia was in her element.

She had seen Clive again last night, when there had been an orchestral concert at the Palace.

She thought how incredibly handsome he was and how different in some ways from the young man who had hidden in Nanny's bed.

Nanny was delighted as well because he had called during the afternoon when she had been the only one in their Apartment.

Alissia had gone out in a barge with her father and the Countess had taken Nancy to attend some gathering in the Royal Palace.

According to Nanny's view, and Nanny was always right as she knew, Clive was even finer and better-looking than the King himself.

She was flushed and excited with all the kind things he had said to her and he had given her a present, which she mentioned only to Alissia.

In a way Alissia was glad she had not been there to spoil the reunion of Nanny and the young man whose life she had saved.

At the same time she wanted to see Clive herself.

It had been impossible to talk to him at the concert because he was sitting by the King and anyway she and her father were quite some way from them.

However, he had come up to them when everyone was leaving and made some flattering remarks to her father before he turned to Alissia.

Clive had thought to himself she was looking even more beautiful in her evening dress than she had been in her day gown.

Later when Clive and His Majesty went upstairs to his private sitting room, the King remarked,

"I have to decide whose bedroom I go to tonight – "

Clive knew he was speaking of his wife, the Queen, and Barbara Castlemaine.

The King made a wide gesture with his hands as he added,

"Whoever I may choose, it will result in pouts and recriminations by the one who is neglected!"

Clive had laughed because he could not help it.

"I am seriously sorry for you, Sire, but it is a puzzle no one can solve except yourself!"

"And I am quite incapable of solving it, Clive," the King chuckled.

When Clive said goodnight and went back to his own Apartment, he was thinking that he did not envy the King.

He himself was glad that he was not married.

He had been hounded, begged and implored by his family to take a wife and thus make sure of an heir to the Marquisate.

If he did not have a son the title would go to some obscure cousin in Surrey, who was getting on in years and, failing him, the title would die out.

"You must be sensible, Clive," one of his relations had said, "and realise it is your responsibility to carry on the title which after all is a very ancient one."

"I am aware of that," he had replied. "But naturally I do not wish to marry until I am in love."

The relative had then looked at him in surprise as if it was the last thing he had expected him to say.

"But surely, Clive, you must realise that you have to marry someone of our own rank," his grandmother had lectured him on frequent occasions, "and preferably a bride with a large dowry."

It was just what the King had said to him so often and Clive was growing tired of hearing it.

The Queen was soft, gentle and apparently already devoted to her husband and yet she had made a scene when she first encountered Barbara Castlemaine.

There was no doubt at all that Barbara was causing confrontations day after day until the King was weary of them.

Equally he had a great affection for her that Clive realised was very sincere.

What was more she had borne him a son and he felt responsible for her.

'The best thing I can do,' Clive said to himself as he climbed into bed, 'is to remain a bachelor. When I am older and my hair is going grey, I will perhaps marry to produce an heir, but until then I intend to enjoy myself.'

He spoke to himself defiantly – as if the very walls of his bedroom were talking to him, as his relations had, of his duty towards his family.

He told himself somewhat cynically before he went to sleep, that if he 'played the field', he would find it far more enjoyable than being tied to one woman.

If he did finally marry, his wife would doubtless be jealous of every woman who even looked at him.

When he saw Alissia and her father at the concert, he had greeted them affectionately.

Alissia had said to him in her sweet gentle voice,

"I have a favour to ask of you, Clive. Please do not think I am a bore, but I do want to see you and His Majesty playing tennis."

Clive had expected something quite different.

"Of course you can. I will tell the gatekeeper at the tennis court that you are always to be admitted and there will be no trouble. But I should tell you that His Majesty and I are playing at six o'clock tomorrow morning."

"I will be there, and thank you, thank you," Alissia sighed. "It is a game I have always wanted to watch."

"Then I will certainly try to beat my opponent," he smiled.

He was about to say more when the King beckoned him and he had to leave.

"Goodnight, my Lord," he turned to Bruce, "I am anxious to have a long talk with you as soon as possible. I need your advice."

"I am always at your service," replied Bruce.

And then Clive had hurried off to obey the King's command.

Alissia gave a little jump for joy.

"I have been longing to watch them play tennis," she enthused, "and I do know that His Majesty plays very early because he dislikes an audience, but I will hide in a corner so that he will not notice me."

"I am sure he will not mind your being there even if he does see you," her father added. "I am told that Clive is a very good player too."

*

Alissia was ready long before it was six o'clock the following morning.

She watched from the window till she saw the King and Clive walking together towards the tennis court.

She gave them a little time to start playing, feeling that she would not be noticed if they were intent on their game.

Then she went to the gate.

The gatekeeper, who was under strict orders to keep everyone else out, smiled at her.

"His Lordship said you'd be comin', my Lady," he said, "and there be plenty of seats to choose from."

Alissia laughed.

"I will make myself as inconspicuous as possible."

She did this by sitting a long way back where she had an excellent view and yet she was not near enough for them to suspect that she was there.

She saw her father was so right in saying that Clive was an exceptionally good player.

At the same time the King was equally proficient.

The game was even until the King won on the very last rally and Alissia suspected that Clive had allowed His Majesty to do so.

The King was delighted at his success and he was smiling as he and Clive walked towards the court door.

It was only then that they became aware that there was a spectator present.

As they both stood looking up at Alissia she hurried down and made a low curtsy to the King.

"I hope you enjoyed the game, Alissia," said Clive.

"It was *very* exciting and I thought that both you and His Majesty played brilliantly. I have always wanted to watch tennis and now it has actually happened to me."

Both men laughed.

"We cannot possibly ask for a greater compliment," remarked the King. "Of course we are grateful for such an appreciative audience. But please do not talk about it, or we will have a large number of busy-bodies staring down at us and doubtless giving us instructions as to how to play better!"

"I think it would be impossible for them to do that," Alissia replied. "And, Your Majesty, I promise that no one will know I have had such a wonderful privilege of being able to watch you both play."

The King smiled and then he and Clive hurried out of the court to change as he had an urgent appointment for immediately after breakfast.

Alissia went back to her own Apartment.

It was unfortunate that, as she was going to her own bedroom, her stepmother came out of her room.

"Why are you up so early?" she asked suspiciously.

"It is such a lovely day, Stepmama. The sun woke me and I thought it was a shame to stay indoors – "

As her stepmother seemed unconvinced, she added,

"You forget I am a country girl."

"Yes indeed you are," the Countess retorted, "and it strikes me that you would be far happier if you went back home to Worcestershire instead of wasting all your time in London."

"I will go back when Papa does."

She saw by the expression on her stepmother's face that this was not the answer she wanted.

There was little doubt that her father was enjoying himself in London after having been in the country for so long – there were only a few people there of his own age or distinction to talk to and he therefore appreciated every moment of his stay at the Royal Palace.

He had always been exceedingly popular with his contemporaries when at school and later when he was in London as a bachelor.

When everything had changed so drastically under the Cromwellians, he had certainly missed the men he had been brought up with.

It had at times been very dull in the country and at others times nerve-wracking when he was scared of doing anything that might attract the attention of the enemy.

Now he was in his element.

There was never any moment of any day, Alissia reckoned, when someone was not either knocking on their door or sending a servant to say her father was wanted in another part of the Royal Palace.

*

After the tennis match she thought she would take Jimbo for a walk in the Park.

The King's dogs would have gone there earlier and there was nothing to see except the ducks on the river.

So she sat down on a bench to watch them.

She was thinking how pretty they looked when she was suddenly joined by Lord Pronett.

She had not heard him approaching the bench and as he unexpectedly sat beside her, she felt a little shiver go through her almost before she realised who he was.

"Her Ladyship informed me that this is where you were likely to be found," he began, "and I would like to talk to you."

"I often come here because it makes it easy for me to think," replied Alissia. "I really enjoy the silence in the Park."

"How charming for you," quipped Freddie, "but I really want to ask you which pictures you would think His Majesty would like to add to his collection."

Alissia looked at him in complete surprise as it was something she had not expected him to say.

She had not thought of him in connection with art.

"I don't think you know," continued Freddie, "that when I came to London I brought with me a Van Dyck and a Holbein as a present for the King. They have been in my family for years, but I felt, as those appalling Cromwellians had sold the Royal Art Collection, his need was somewhat greater than mine."

"That was so kind of you, Lord Pronett. My father has told me how hard the King has been working to replace the collection he had lost. It was yet another wicked thing those horrible Cromwellians did."

"I agree with you, Alissia, but I have quite a lot of pictures at home that I feel would be giving more pleasure to people if they were here in the Royal Palace than they are at the moment in the depths of Norfolk."

"Is that where you live?" Alissia asked him.

"That is where my home is, but I am thinking of buying a house in London and I would like to ask you your advice on that subject too."

Alissia laughed.

"I am afraid you have come to the wrong person. I have lived in the country all my life until we came here to the Coronation and everything is thrilling to me. I want to see far more of London than I have seen yet."

"Then you must let me show you around."

Alissia shook her head.

"No, I am intending to go with my Papa. He is very knowledgeable about houses, and of course, he grew up in London and lived here except when he was at school."

"I have a great admiration for your father," Freddie said, "but even more for his very beautiful daughter."

Alissia did not understand quite why, but somehow his compliment made her feel strangely uncomfortable.

She had received many compliments since coming to London and she was actually beginning to take them as a matter of course.

But there was something unpleasant about the way Lord Pronett paid his or maybe it was the man himself.

She felt strongly that there was something wrong about him, yet she could not put a name to it.

She rose to her feet.

"I must go back to the Palace, my Lord, I am sure there are things waiting for me there which I have to do, although I have for the moment forgotten what they are."

"Then keep on forgetting them, Alissia. Stay here and talk to me. I have been longing to be alone with you, but somehow you have always managed to evade me."

Alissia did not answer him.

And then he expanded,

"Need I tell you just how beautiful you are and how really exciting it is for me to meet someone I really admire for the first time in my life. Someone who from the first moment I set eyes on her made me aware that she was the only woman in the world I really wanted to know."

He was speaking with what seemed to be a great deal of emotion and yet somehow Alissia felt it was what he had been planning to say.

There was something missing in the way he spoke and in what he said.

None of it was genuine or spontaneous.

It was as if he had thought out his little speech very carefully in advance.

Maybe her stepmother had told him what to say.

Impulsively Alissia jumped to her feet.

"I am sorry to appear rude, my Lord, but I have to get back to the Royal Palace and Jimbo wants a run."

She walked away so quickly that before he could even think about rising to his feet, she was almost flying down the footpath and out through the gate of the Park.

He looked after her in surprise and then he gave a laugh.

He thought that she must be frightened of him and it amused him to think that anyone so lovely, so beautiful and so glorious should be afraid of Freddie Brown.

Then he told himself that all young women desired a title.

And as the Countess had pointed out to him, Alissia was very young and unspoilt.

It was the Countess's idea that he should marry her and for a moment he had laughed when she suggested it.

On his way to London as the new Lord Pronett with a considerable amount of money at his disposal, he had thought of the many things he might say and do.

He had rehearsed in his mind a thousand times what he would say to the King.

And yet it had never really occurred to him that at his age he should get married.

A wife, however, could easily be a great advantage to him in the social life he craved.

The moment he had made himself Lord Pronett he had wanted above everything else to discuss the affairs of State with Courtiers and politicians.

He knew that all those following the King regularly did so and he was sure the 'open sesame' for him had been the two pictures he had brought for the King's collection.

He could trust his native cunning to smooth his way upwards, once he had managed to gain his entrée into the Royal Palace itself.

Everything had gone even more smoothly than he anticipated and he was exceptionally pleased with all that had happened since his arrival.

The King's appreciation of his present of two such significant pictures enabled him to mingle with the Court, who were all distinguished men on their own ground.

When he spoke of the other pictures he owned, they were astounded.

"I had no idea" a Duke had said, "that such a fine collection as you tell us you have has been unnoticed for so long."

"I think all the family have been collectors," replied Freddie in a serious voice. "Only as we are so far away in the country from London you did not hear of us."

"Which was certainly a great blessing in disguise for you," another Courtier came in. "King Charles I was a patron of Rubens and Van Dyck and had a great number of their pictures in his Collection.

"I well remember seeing them!" another Courtier exclaimed. "Then they were all sold off in that disgraceful way by those ghastly followers of Cromwell. But thanks to you, Lord Pronett, we now at least have one Van Dyck and a Holbein!"

"I must talk to His Majesty about the Rubens I have at my home," added Freddie. "And I think he would also be interested in a Velazquez."

He was aware as he spoke that the eyes of the men listening were shining and he knew he was on a very good wicket.

He was not surprised when later in the day the King discussed with him the changes he would like to make at Windsor Castle.

He needed to build some new Apartments there for himself and the Queen and he also told Freddie he wanted to add to the Royal Library.

One thing Freddie had been able to do when he was alone in the house in Norfolk was to read, as his employer was too weak to talk much to him and the servants were not interested.

He had been able to learn about the books in the Royal Collection and who had contributed to beautifying the Royal Palaces over the years.

He would not have known about the magnificent ceiling in the Banqueting Hall in the Palace of Whitehall, which had been built by Inigo Jones in 1622 if he had not read about it before he arrived in London.

He had an excellent memory that had been trained by his father since he was a boy, and thanks to his father he spoke without a provincial accent, even though the children he played with in childhood all had accents which revealed the County they had been brought up in.

Freddie could now see himself settling down in a grand house in London as he definitely wanted to be near the Royal presence and the Courtiers surrounding the King.

He would keep Pronett Hall in Norfolk to supply him with an income from the estate and he could use it as a holiday home if he ever had a family.

'I have my whole scenario planned in great detail now,' Freddie reflected as he went to bed that night.

He congratulated himself on having been so clever as to win the interest of the King through his pictures and to be able to converse with the most cultured of the Court about art.

He knew that the pictures and other items he could sell from Pronett Hall would ensure him a place at Court for the rest of his life.

Of course once he was established he would want to entertain and it was the Countess who had put the idea of marriage so firmly into his head.

She suggested that no one would make him a more attractive or acceptable wife as far as the Royal family was concerned than her husband's daughter by his first wife.

"Alissia is not only very beautiful," she said, "but she is also very intelligent. I can understand so well, Lord Pronett, that you need someone who will appreciate art in the same way as you do yourself."

It was difficult when he received a compliment of this sort for Freddie not to laugh.

He had not taken the slightest notice of the pictures at Pronett Hall for years and then suddenly it had struck him that they were very valuable and could be of great use to him.

When Oliver Cromwell died he had known with a quickness of mind inherited from his real father that he had a passport to King Charles II if he ever returned.

Before Freddie left for London he hurriedly read everything he could find about the pictures in the library at Pronett Hall.

He had, of course, used the library in the long years when he was acting as secretary to Lord Pronett when he had nothing else to do.

It did not take him long to realise the importance of painters such as Rubens and Van Dyck and also Bruegel, Holbein, Titian and a number of other great artists.

But they had never occurred to him as being of any particular relevance to himself.

Now he had brought three volumes of *Histories of Art* with him from the library and he learned from them with the same concentrated attention he had given to his arithmetic as a boy.

However he had at first been overcome by the sheer magnificence of the Royal Palace itself.

The King kept saying there was a great deal to be done to it, but it was difficult for Freddie not to exclaim at everything in sheer astonishment.

It was so completely different from anything he had ever experienced in his life before.

But now his conversation with the Countess had made another idea spring into his head.

He had been so astonished at his own brilliance at impersonating the heir to Lord Pronett and taking over his house and estate – then being accepted without question at Whitehall.

Now he felt as if he was an explorer seeing in the distance something even greater than he had ever imagined previously.

'I will start a family of my own,' Freddie decided, 'and they will be brought up to be Courtiers as I intend to be myself and the most aristocratic ladies in the land will be at their disposal.'

He had carefully thought out every detail before he left Norfolk for London.

He would be of more influence than he had ever dreamed possible when he had made himself Lord Pronett.

There was one point the Countess had made very clear, although she had not actually intended it that way.

It was that he should start a family and his children would naturally all be members of the English aristocracy.

For this he required a wife.

In the sitting room of their Apartment in the Palace of Whitehall, the Countess of Dalwaynnie was, as it so happened, thinking of Lord Pronett.

What she wanted was that he should sweep Alissia away quickly and leave the road open for Nancy to marry the Marquis of Morelanton.

Freddie, if he was to be believed, was very well off with a large estate in Norfolk.

But Clive was entirely different.

His ancestors had become Kings of Scotland in the past and while he lived on the border, he was respected by the Scots as well as the English.

One of his great-aunts had become the Queen of a Scandinavian country and the Countess had been told that his mother had been a Lady of the Royal Bedchamber.

She could easily imagine Nancy eventually taking that place at Court and this she wanted to achieve more than anything else.

In fact there should have been no difficulties at all if it was not for Alissia.

She had only to see her lovely golden hair shining in the sun and to hear Alissia's soft and enchanting voice to know that if she was honest Nancy could not compete with her.

She had found it very difficult when she had first married Bruce not to be jealous of his first wife.

He had obviously adored her and the servants and everyone she met had told her how beautiful she had been and how much she had been loved by everyone with whom she came into contact.

Any woman would have found it difficult to hold her own under such circumstances, but the Countess was persistent in everything she did.

She was quite certain that Bruce really loved her.

He would in fact, she believed, have forgotten his happiness with his first wife were it not for the presence of Alissia.

The Countess had become obsessed with this idea and she thought that every time her husband looked at his daughter and saw how beautiful she was, he was repeating beneath his breath, 'exactly like her mother.'

Nanny did not make it any better by continually referring to her.

She had been told by Bruce to be very careful as to what she said about Elizabeth and to remember that while the Cromwellians were in power she was always plain Mrs. Dalton.

But Nanny had always spoken to the older servants about 'her Ladyship' and she did not change when Lady Hestor arrived.

"Her Ladyship always insisted that we did 'so and so' at this time of year," she would say continually.

She had no idea she was making the new Countess wince.

'Immediately Alissia is married,' she told herself, 'I will get rid of Nanny. I will pension her off and make sure I do the same to all the other servants who have been with my husband for far too long.'

When they came to London, it had been Bruce who had insisted that Nanny should accompany Alissia.

His new wife had protested loudly, but he insisted and once they finally settled in at Whitehall, Nanny took over as she always did.

The servants who were provided for them in the Royal Palace looked to Nanny for their instructions rather than to the Countess.

So every day when she thought it all over, she was more and more determined that Alissia must somehow be rapidly disposed of.

If she was not around, the Countess was sure that Clive would feel it his duty to marry Nancy – if only as a thank-offering to Bruce for saving his life.

Instinctively, although she could really not explain it, she was quite certain that Lord Pronett was determined to marry into the aristocracy.

He spoke of himself as having many generations of an aristocratic family behind him, but she had to admit that she had never heard of the Pronetts before.

But there was little reason why she should have as she had lived in a very different part of England.

At the same time she was sure that the Pronetts had not shone at any stage in history or for that matter had been very well known, as he now said, for their art collection.

However he was a young man, quite nice looking and socially ambitious.

What could be more to his advantage than if he was to marry the daughter of the Earl of Dalwaynnie?

Naturally she had heard the full story on the Palace grapevine that he had so generously given two outstanding pictures to the King.

She had even made that the excuse for discussing with Freddie the pictures in their country house and asking his advice.

"I am sure my husband does not want to sell them," she said lightly. "Equally I do think they should be insured if they are really valuable. I have heard you are an expert on the great artists, Lord Pronett, so therefore you must tell me what you think the value might be of our pictures in the country."

"Of course," Freddie replied. "I would be only too delighted to help your Ladyship. If you give me a list of the pictures and who they are painted by, I will be glad to mark those that I think should be kept safely not only from burglars, but also from too much sunlight or neglect of any sort."

"You are so kind," the Countess cooed. "So please come to us this evening when I have talked to my husband about it. I know he will be grateful to you for taking such an interest in his possessions, which I rather suspect have been neglected and taken for granted in the past."

Freddie laughed.

"That happens with a great number of collections," he responded. "In fact several gentlemen of the Court have told me that their finest pictures have been damaged simply by neglect."

He saw the Countess was impressed and continued,

"I feel they are all part of our heritage so we should not only enjoy them but make absolutely certain they are not taken from us or damaged inadvertently."

"Of course you are right," the Countess agreed with a look of admiration. "If only everyone was as sensible as you. The Duke of Hamilton was saying to me only a short while ago that all his pictures need cleaning. The Duke of Richmond said much the same about his collection."

Freddie drew in his breath – this was just the sort of company he wished to keep.

He was well aware that the Countess was doing her best to impress him.

He was in little doubt as to why she was doing so and finally with a sigh she said,

"I find I have so little time to enjoy the arts because I have two girls to chaperone. I only hope when they are both married that I will have more time for myself."

"I am sure you will," Freddie murmured because it was expected of him.

"My stepdaughter, Alissia, is not just beautiful but is also particularly interested in art. She draws and paints quite well and you will find she knows a good deal about the great Masters."

There was silence for a minute and then she added,

"I am sure you already know that in marriage it is so important for the two people to have the same interests. It is something my father always said to me. When I first met my husband we were drawn to each other by the fact that we both loved the country and he was very keen on his horses."

There was silence and Freddie was wondering what he should say now before her Ladyship cantered on,

"One day you will marry and I can only hope that you will find a woman who is as interested in art as you are. As I have already told you, it is a great interest of my stepdaughter's.

"And as you must admit she looks herself as if she has just stepped off a canvas painted by one of the great Masters!"

Surely Alissia could be the foundation stone of the great family he was to build in the future – a Pronett family which would echo endlessly down the ages.

Not only for their blue blood but for their collection of art which if he was clever would draw him closer and ever closer into the Royal Family.

CHAPTER SIX

Alissia woke late the next morning because she had attended a party in the Royal Palace that had gone on until the early hours.

She had enjoyed every moment, especially dancing with Clive.

She had hoped every time she had seen him that he would dance with her as he had done with Nancy, and that was when he had not known she was in the Royal Palace.

But at last her dream had come true.

As she expected he was an excellent dancer and he looked overwhelmingly handsome in his evening attire.

Alissia was too modest to realise how beautiful she looked herself.

It was a large party arranged by the King and she had therefore chosen the prettiest gown from her wardrobe as it became her more than any of the others.

It was white, but there were many diamante sewn into the lace and satin of the dress which shimmered when she walked.

Her father was the first to compliment her,

"I am very proud of you tonight, my darling. You look so unbelievably lovely."

"I hoped you would think so, Papa."

She was aware that her stepmother had overheard her father's words.

There was a distinctly unpleasant look in her eyes as she tossed her head and walked on without speaking.

Whatever her stepmother might feel, Alissia was determined to enjoy herself.

She realised that she had been deliberately kept away from such parties when they first came to the Royal Palace, but now she was determined to make up for it.

The music was perfect and no one could have been a better or more charming host than the King, who was insistent that everyone should enjoy themselves as much as he.

He walked round all the guests paying the women compliments and exchanging jokes with the men.

The food was the finest that the chefs could supply and the great ballroom with its innumerable candles made everything seem as if it was part of a glorious dream.

It was two o'clock in the morning before Alissia finally put her head down on her pillow, but before she fell asleep she felt that once again she was dancing round and round the great ballroom with Clive.

*

When she awoke she realised that it was well after six o'clock.

She had meant to watch the King and Clive playing tennis again.

They told her last night that was what they intended to do and the King had assured her,

"You are a very quiet and good audience, Alissia, therefore we are delighted to see you and as I asked you before please don't tell anyone in the Palace. Otherwise we will have a permanent audience and it will distract us from our game."

"I have been very careful already, Your Majesty," Alissia replied.

He smiled at her and patted her shoulder.

"You look very beautiful tonight, Alissia, and I am not in the least surprised that all the gentlemen of the Court want to dance with you – "

He laughed as he added,

"And all the women are jealous!"

He mouthed the last words in almost a whisper and Alissia blushed.

The King thought as he went away that he had been right in thinking that she was exceptionally lovely and that she was definitely an asset to the Royal Palace.

He had decided when he was in exile that he would make his Palace more glamorous and more attractive than any other Royal Palace on the Continent.

He knew that depended a great deal on the women and he was thus determined, now he was in power, that he would invite as his guests only the loveliest women in his Kingdom.

He would also encourage his Courtiers to marry ladies who would be an asset to the Royal parties.

Barbara Castlemaine played up to his wishes, not just because it was what he wanted but she inevitably made herself look her best on every possible occasion.

She had a definite flair for looking fantastic.

The King had been the first to declare that she was amazingly beautiful and it proved impossible for him to do the right thing and give up Barbara.

Especially as she had given birth to one child of his, and he suspected she was starting another.

It was extremely difficult for any man to keep two women contented under such circumstances and yet on the whole the King was amazingly successful.

His wife, the Queen, already adored him and she wanted to please him in every way she possibly could. She was clearly jealous of Barbara and who indeed could have expected her to be anything else.

At the same time she realised that because she was the Queen, she had the upper hand.

Therefore she did not directly ask her husband to send his Mistress away and she had an uneasy feeling he would not do so even if she asked.

She barely bit back the words that came to her lips and in the end managed to persuade herself that Barbara was not present even when she was.

Fortunately Alissia was not in the least worried by such problems.

She just wanted to dance, to enjoy the music and the beauty of the Royal Palace ballroom.

She danced so gracefully that almost every man present watched her and it seemed as if her feet hardly touched the floor.

Her eyes were shining with enjoyment, appearing to reflect the candles themselves.

*

Once Alissia realised how late it was, she jumped up, washed herself and dressed hurriedly.

Because she was going to see the King and Clive she put on one of her prettiest day gowns and took a great deal of trouble over her hair.

Then she whistled for Jimbo who was asleep under her bed.

They ran down the stairs together and out through a side door into the yard. The gate to the tennis court was at the far end by the stairs.

She was hurrying on towards it when suddenly she saw Lord Pronett in front of her.

Standing beside him was a man who seemed to be dressed as a sailor.

Lord Pronett was directly in her way and she could not avoid him.

"Good morning, Alissia," he trumpeted, sweeping off his hat. "I was wondering what had happened to you, as I understood from Nancy that you were always up very early."

"I am so behindhand this morning," smiled Alissia, "because we were very late last night at the ball."

She was anxious to move on as she did not like to say that she was going to the tennis court as it would reveal her secret to Lord Pronett that she was allowed to watch His Majesty play.

"I want you to come with me," said Lord Pronett rather aggressively "to inspect a ship that is waiting just below us."

"I would love to see it another time, my Lord, and thank you for the invitation. But I must now exercise my dog."

She caught hold of Jimbo as she spoke in case he should run ahead of her into the tennis court and fixed the lead she was carrying in her hand on the collar round his neck.

"Jimbo must wait!" replied Lord Pronett. "I insist that you come and see the ship now as it is waiting for you on the Thames."

Alissia was going to protest again.

Then to her astonishment, the sailor, who had been standing back as Lord Pronett was speaking to her, moved forward and stood closely on the other side of her.

As he did so Lord Pronett reached out his hand as if he intended to hold her arm so that she could not escape.

"Surely," she suggested a little hesitantly, "I can see your ship a little later. I really want to go in the Park with Jimbo – straight away."

"You are coming to see the ship *now*," Lord Pronett persisted firmly. "What I have to show you cannot wait."

There was something in the sharpness of his voice that intimidated Alissia.

Then even as she thought frantically what she could do, there was a sound of dogs barking and yelping.

The King's dogs came out of the Palace escorted by their keeper.

"If I am coming with you," Alissia said quickly to Lord Pronett, "then I must leave Jimbo with the other dogs. You will not want him on the ship."

Before Lord Pronett could reply she slipped away from him, dragging Jimbo with her and this prevented the sailor from stopping her.

Then she ran as quickly as she could towards the King's dogs and their keeper, Bill.

As she reached him she could see that the sailor and Lord Pronett were running behind her.

She slipped through the dogs and placing the end of Jimbo's lead into Bill's hand, she said in a whisper that only he could hear,

"I am being kidnapped by Lord Pronett. *Please* tell Lord Morelanton to come and save me."

Bill stared at her in amazement.

She had only just uttered her appeal when the sailor reached her and grabbed her arm in his.

"His Lordship be waitin' for you, lady," he grunted in a hard uneducated voice.

Pulling her away from the dogs, he then dragged her towards Lord Pronett who had moved on.

They had nearly reached the steps that led down to the Thames, when Alissia demanded.

"What is happening? Where are you taking me?"

Neither of the men answered as Lord Pronett strode ahead and still holding on to her painfully, the sailor pulled Alissia behind him.

Then she saw the gangway of a ship waiting ahead of them. It was not a particularly large ship, but she knew from its three masts, which were unusually high, that it was a swift vessel.

There was no time for her to speak or protest or even pretend that she was interested in the ship.

Lord Pronett walked up the gangway and onto the deck and because the sailor still had a firm hold of her and he was undoubtedly a strong man, Alissia had no choice but to follow him.

As soon as they were aboard the ship, the gangway was pulled in and the oarsmen below began dipping their oars into the water.

Still pulling Alissia by the arm, the sailor followed Lord Pronett into a cabin just below the centre of the ship.

Even as she was pushed into the cabin and the door was closed, she felt the ship beginning to move.

Lord Pronett was standing at the porthole looking out.

As he turned round, Alissia screamed at him,

"What are you doing? Why have you brought me here in such an extraordinary manner and forced me onto this ship? And where are we going?"

"We are going to my estate in Norfolk, Alissia, my dear. When we arrive we will be married."

Alissia stared at him in astonishment.

"*Married*?" she exclaimed. "I have not the slightest intention whatever of marrying you!"

"It is what your stepmother desires and I am very eager, I can assure you, to be your husband – "

Alissia tried her very best to keep calm, but it was becoming increasingly difficult.

"But I have no wish, my Lord, to be your wife. Nor would I marry a man I hardly know and do not love."

"I will make you love me," he insisted without too much conviction.

"That would be impossible. I have never liked you since I first saw you and, to be truthful, I would rather *die* than marry you!"

Lord Pronett looked at her as if he could hardly believe what she was saying.

"Is that clear?" continued Alissia. "Now take me back to the Royal Palace at once"

"I will do nothing of the sort. Your stepmother said you will make me a good wife and I intend to make you a very good husband. We will therefore be married as soon as we arrive and I think you will enjoy being the chatelaine of my large house."

"I have told you already that I refuse to marry you," Alissia shrieked angrily. "And if you persist in trying to make me, I will throw myself into the sea!"

"This is ridiculous," Lord Pronett growled. "If you will listen to me, I will tell you how happy I will make you and how pleasant it will be for you to be my wife."

"*I hate you*," retorted Alissia. "It is shocking and wicked of you to carry me away in this appalling fashion. My father will be furious, not only with you but with my stepmother for thinking up such an absurd idea."

She realised as she raged on that Lord Pronett was looking astonished – it was as if he had never anticipated for a single moment that this could possibly be her reaction to his proposal.

As he did not answer, Alissia ran to the porthole.

It was open and she looked out.

They were moving down the Thames quite swiftly and she guessed that when they reached the middle of the river, the current would carry them quicker still.

She could see a number of people walking on the embankment and she wondered if she screamed out loudly whether they would try to rescue her.

Then as the ship gathered speed she knew that they would only stare and anyway there would be no way for them to reach her.

She felt really terrified as well as angry by what was happening to her.

She thought that Lord Pronett was an evil monster waiting to destroy her.

*

Alissia had only just been dragged down the steps to the ship when, having finished their game, the King and Clive came out through the tennis court gate.

Clive had won the game handsomely this morning and the King was blaming the large amount of wine he had consumed last night.

"I beat you yesterday," he asserted, "when I had had little or nothing to drink the night before. I am quite certain it was the heavy wine they were serving last night which enabled you to humiliate me this morning."

"I had to fight hard for my victory," smiled Clive. "Tomorrow Your Majesty will undoubtedly be the winner if you abstain at dinner time!"

"I will take great care that *you* are offered the finest and heaviest wine in my cellar!" replied the King.

They were both laughing as they reached the dogs who jumped up affectionately at Clive as well as the King.

As he bent down to pat one dog that was clawing at his knee, he exclaimed,

"Why, it's Jimbo! What is he doing here?"

"His Mistress, my Lord, has only just 'anded 'im to me," Bill then piped up, "and she asked me to tell your Lordship that she were bein' kidnapped by Lord Pronett."

Clive stared at him.

"*What did you say?*" he asked the man.

"That be what she said, my Lord, and Lord Pronett and a man as looked as if 'e'd just come off a ship 'ave dragged 'er down the steps to the river."

"Dragged her!"

"She says they were kidnappin' 'er, my Lord, and that's what I thinks meself they were a-doin'."

Clive looked at the King who had heard what the dog keeper had just said.

"You had better see what this is all about, Clive," he suggested. "It all sounds very odd to me."

"And to me, Sire."

Even as he spoke he saw that Nancy was standing on the top of the steps that led down to the river.

Clive then hurried towards her and saw that she was watching a ship moving speedily downstream.

"What is happening here?" he asked Nancy sharply. "Is it true that Alissia has been taken away on that ship you are watching?"

"Yes, that's right," replied Nancy sulkily.

"By Lord Pronett?"

Nancy nodded.

"It was my Mama's idea. I heard her telling him to take her away and marry her."

"I don't believe it!" exclaimed Clive, "why should she do such a thing?"

"Because Mama wants *you* to marry *me*," Nancy answered even more sulkily. "She reckoned Alissia was stopping you from doing so."

"I have no intention of marrying anyone and I don't want to marry you, so you need not even think about it."

"And I do not want to marry you," pouted Nancy.

And then she added surprisingly,

"I would love to marry Lord Pronett!"

Clive looked at her.

"Then what we have to do is to save your stepsister from what will undoubtedly be a very unhappy marriage if it is ever allowed to take place."

"How can we do that?" Nancy asked petulantly.

As she spoke Clive had taken her by the hand and was pulling her down the steps leading to the river.

Just to the right of them was the Royal Barge that was always on guard at that particular point in the river whenever the King was in residence in the Royal Palace.

As Clive well knew that it was built for war and its canon were of the very latest and most effective type.

The Royal Barge had obviously been up river and had just moored beside the Palace facing downstream.

Moving swiftly up the gangway Clive leapt aboard and then he turned round to help Nancy jump in after him.

The Captain of the Royal Barge emerged from the quarter-deck and walked towards him.

"I am the Marquis of Morelanton," Clive declared, holding out his hand, "and I have His Majesty's orders that you should now overtake and board a particular ship that is already hurrying downriver."

The Captain, who had saluted him politely and then taken his hand, was obviously delighted.

"I'll give the orders immediately, my Lord. Have you any idea the name of the ship?"

"Miss Gordon, who is here with me now and saw the ship leave, will identify it. How many oarsmen have you?"

The Captain smiled.

"Twenty-four, my Lord, and with my men I don't believe there's a ship in the Thames that could equal us, let alone beat us!"

"Then let's get started!" urged Clive.

"Aye, aye, my Lord!"

The Captain gave his orders and the oarsmen below who had been in the process of shipping their oars now pushed them out again.

By this time Lord Pronett's ship carrying Alissia was out of sight.

It was not until they were well past the Tower of London that Nancy gave a cry and pointed downriver.

"There it is," she shouted, "but it's still a long way ahead of us."

Clive turned to the Captain.

"I think it would be a mistake for us to go too far out to sea, Captain."

"We are already breaking our record for setting sail, my Lord, and I promise yon ship will not escape us."

The wind was now filling the tall sails of the Royal Barge and Clive was aware that the oarsmen were rowing very effectively.

However, Lord Pronett's ship was also fast and its Captain was obviously intelligent enough to keep it in the strong current running towards the sea.

It was only with extreme effort by the crew of the Royal Barge and the skill of its Captain that they managed eventually to overtake their quarry.

Nancy once again assured Clive that Alissia was on board, but there was no sign of her or of Lord Pronett on deck.

Then the Captain of the Royal Barge shouted out to the Captain of Lord Pronett's ship to draw into the bank.

The ship, which Clive guessed had been hired by Lord Pronett, slowed and then it seemed reluctantly pulled over.

There was no question of their not obeying and the Captain was obviously overawed by the sudden arrival of the heavily armed Royal Barge.

Slowly he steered his ship out of the middle of the river to where the water was much shallower.

The Royal Barge moved alongside Lord Pronett's ship, which was now pressed against the riverbank.

Clive then jumped athletically from the deck of the Royal Barge and onto the deck of Lord Pronett's ship.

There was still no sign anywhere of either Alissia or Lord Pronett.

As the Captain walked cautiously across the deck towards him, Clive asked sharply,

"Where is Lord Pronett?"

Speaking in a surly manner the Captain, who was obviously a rough type, pointed with a dirty finger.

"He be in the cabin below deck."

Clive did not wait to hear anymore.

He merely turned round and found his way, because he was often at sea and the layout of all ships was much the same.

He opened the door of the cabin, which was below the deck and in the stern of the ship.

Seated in an armchair, Alissia was at the far end of the cabin and Lord Pronett was at the porthole wondering why they were not moving.

Alissia saw Clive first.

She gave out a little cry as she jumped up from her chair.

She ran towards him and flung herself against him.

"You have come!" she breathed. *"Save me!* Please take me away, Clive, I am so very terrified."

Clive put his arms round her.

He found as he held her that her whole body was trembling against his.

Then, as his arms tightened and he looked down at her frightened pleading face, he knew that he loved her.

"It's all right, my darling," he said softly.

Then without releasing her, he turned towards Lord Pronett.

"What the devil are you up to, Pronett?" he cried. "And where are you taking Alissia?"

Lord Pronett had been staring at him ever since he had burst into the cabin.

Now he said in a shaking voice that did not sound like his own,

"How did you get here? How did you find us?"

"Never mind that, Pronett. How dare you abduct Alissia from the Royal Palace? Surely you must realise that if she now appeals to His Majesty, you would surely be sentenced to imprisonment in the Tower of London for many years."

Lord Pronett looked at him in horror.

"You – cannot – mean that," he stammered.

"I certainly do, Pronett, and if you have hurt her in any way, I will have you shot, you blackguard!"

Lord Pronett held out his hands.

"I – merely arranged with her stepmother – to take her to my home – and marry her," he blathered.

Clive looked at him and then at Alissia.

Her face was hidden in his shoulder.

"Listen," he said softly, "Nancy is up on deck and I want you to go up and join her. I promise I will take you home, Alissia, but I just want a word with Lord Pronett before I do so."

"You will not – let him – take me away," Alissia asked him in a petrified whisper.

"You know I will not, Alissia, and I will take you back as soon as I have dealt with him and I promise you this will never happen to you again."

She glanced up at him and he thought no woman could look so lovely.

For a moment it was very hard to take his eyes from hers.

Then as she obediently left the cabin, Clive shut the door behind her.

"I was intending when I caught you," he growled, "to give you a good thrashing and it would be something you would always remember."

Lord Pronett shuddered, but he did not speak.

"Now I really want to know, Pronett, why you did something so obviously absurd as to kidnap a girl who you well know is under the protection of His Majesty."

There was still no answer from Lord Pronett and Clive continued,

"If you really meant to marry her against her will, any fool would know that you would be creating a hell on earth for yourself."

For a moment Clive thought that Lord Pronett was still not going to reply.

Then he answered in a timid and hesitating voice,

"I thought – every woman wanted – to be married to a man – with a title."

Clive stared at him as if he found it hard to believe that he had actually said anything so patently ridiculous.

Then wiping his forehead Lord Pronett added,

"I really had no idea – it would upset her. I thought she would be pleased and flattered, but when she said that she would – kill herself rather than be married to me – I honestly did not know what to do about it."

"You must be incredibly naïve and stupid, Pronett, if you think that anyone as beautiful and lovely as Alissia would ever marry a man she hardly knew and who from all accounts she does not particularly like."

"I told her I would make her love me," wailed Lord Pronett, "although I was not quite certain – how I could do so."

There was a brief silence and then Clive asked him,

"How many women have you made love to?"

Again there was silence.

And then Lord Pronett admitted,

"I have been living in the country for the last five years looking after my – father – who was seriously ill and therefore we could not entertain."

He stammered over the word 'father', but the rest of what he said seemed to come naturally.

He had no idea that for a moment Clive had felt like laughing.

Then to his own surprise Clive began to feel a little sorry for Lord Pronett.

He had been somewhat suspicious since he first met Lord Pronett that he was a social climber and had thought him someone of no influence who could be safely ignored.

Yet now Lord Pronett had actually admitted that Alissia's feelings had to be considered too.

Aloud he said,

"When I came aboard, I meant to knock you down and teach you a lesson you would not forget in a hurry. You would doubtless attempt to defend yourself, but, as I am more athletic that you are, I could undoubtedly have beaten you into insensibility."

Lord Pronett drew in his breath, but again he was sensible enough to say nothing.

"Now I realise," Clive went on, "that you have just made a mess of something, which was far too big for you to even contemplate let alone put into action effectively."

"If you are talking of my marriage to Alissia," Lord Pronett said, "it was her stepmother who suggested it."

Clive knew that this was true from what Nancy had told him already.

"For a marriage to be happy," he continued, "it has to depend on the two people concerned loving each other. I can understand you wanted to marry into the aristocracy to make certain of your position at the Royal Court. But it is something that you could never have achieved with a wife who hated you."

"I can appreciate that – now," Lord Pronett replied, "but I swear to you, I thought because her stepmother said all girls wanted to be married, she would accept me – and we would build up – a family that would make my name a proud one – in the years to come."

He stumbled a little over his words, but Clive felt that he was speaking with a degree of sincerity.

"Very well, Pronett, I accept your explanation and I will not punish you as I intended when I came on board."

He thought that Lord Pronett gave a sigh of relief and then he added,

"Yet if, as you say, you want to settle down and raise a family, then why not marry a girl who is already attracted to you and who will ensure, I am quite certain, your place at Court."

Lord Pronett stared at him.

He did not understand and Clive explained,

"I am talking about Nancy. She is not as beautiful as Alissia, but she's a very pleasant, well-behaved and well brought-up young woman. She told me her mother wished her to marry me, but she would far rather marry *you*."

Lord Pronett still stared at him as if he could not have heard right.

"Did she say so?" he asked.

"She did, and I know she was frightened all the way here that we might not be in time to stop you marrying her stepsister."

Clive could see a light growing in Lord Pronett's eyes and he carried on,

"I can imagine nothing that would help you more to establish yourself and your future family at Court. You may not know that the Countess's first cousin is the Duke of Devonshire and her family tree is one of the longest and most important in the whole of the country."

Now Lord Pronett was listening to him intently.

"The Countess just like all mothers has exaggerated ideas of her daughter's attractiveness. But after all you have a large house in the country and I understand enough money to buy yourself a fine one in London."

Lord Pronett nodded to show that this was true.

"Start your family with Nancy," suggested Clive, "and you will find there are very few people in the Court circle who will not respect you and then be proud of your friendship."

He thought the light that now shone in Freddie's eyes was somehow rather pathetic.

But he had made his point and he knew that Freddie would only be too pleased to take his advice.

"Now what I suggest, Pronett, is that having hired this ship to carry you to Norfolk, you marry Nancy before her mother can interfere and say you are not good enough for her. And I will take Alissia back to the Royal Palace with me."

"Do you really think – that Nancy will come with – me," Lord Pronett asked rather humbly.

"You may have to beg her on your knees to be your wife, but I don't think you will find it is as difficult as you anticipate. I am certain she will make you a charming wife and one who will please His Majesty the King."

Clive smiled before he added,

"While he will surely give you a wedding present, I suggest you bring him another exceptionally fine picture from your own collection."

He noticed as he was speaking that Lord Pronett was staring intently at him – it was as if he could hardly believe what was happening to him.

He seemed almost afraid that he would suddenly wake up and find it had been a dream.

"What I am going to do now," declared Clive, "is to send Nancy down to you and leave you to persuade her to take Alissia's place. In fact to marry you as soon as you reach Norfolk."

"Supposing she says 'no'?" Lord Pronett asked.

Clive gave a laugh.

"That is up to you. I can suggest what I think will make you happy, but I cannot do your wooing for you!"

"No, of course not. I can only thank you for being so kind and for understanding that I did not mean to harm Alissia."

"You did what many men have done before now. You listened to a woman who was jealous and who wanted to run your life her way rather than the way you wanted it yourself.

"Now stay where you are while I send Nancy down to you. Good luck to you, Pronett, and I hope you will find the happiness we all seek one way or another."

He did not wait for Lord Pronett to reply as he went out of the cabin closing the door behind him.

Outside Clive found the two girls standing looking at the ships and barges going up and down the river.

Nancy was aware of his approach first and turned round quickly.

"I want to speak to you, Nancy – "

He then drew her to one side so that Alissia could not hear what they were saying.

"Lord Pronett," he began, "is extremely upset that he should have frightened Alissia. He was only carrying out your mother's instructions. I hope you will forgive me for saying that her plan was very foolish and, as it happens, extremely unkind to him."

"Unkind?" Nancy queried.

"I think Lord Pronett is attracted to you, but your mother did not think that he was good enough for you. She therefore planned to take him out of the picture as far as you were concerned and at the same time ridding her of Alissia, who she was afraid might marry me."

Clive noticed that Nancy was listening attentively to every word.

"What I would like you to do is to comfort him and forgive him for being a fool. He knows now that is what he has been for listening to your mother and not following his heart, as he really should have done."

"You mean," Nancy asked in a small voice, "that he cares for *me*?"

"I think that is what he will tell you, but you must find out for yourself. You should realise that a man must never be hurt. Not only in his feelings but in his pride in himself. That is what has happened to Lord Pronett at this very moment."

Nancy made a little sound, but Clive went on,

"So what I suggest you do is to go down and cheer him up. If you feel inclined to be brave and do what he suggests, I think you might both find great happiness."

He saw Nancy's eyes widen.

Then, as if she found it impossible to answer him, she turned and ran towards the door that led down to the cabin.

Clive walked over to where Alissia was standing.

She was still gazing out at the ships and barges on the river.

As he reached her, she looked up at him.

He thought that the question mark in her eyes and the pleading in her face made her look even lovelier than ever.

Her look made him feel that she needed him and in return he knew how much he needed her.

"Now we are going back," he said. "We have done what we came to do, and I think Lord Pronett and Nancy have much to say to each other. So we must not interfere."

As he finished speaking he did not wait for Alissia to reply.

He walked quickly over to where the two Captains were standing on the quarter-deck talking to each other.

They were obviously waiting for orders.

"Lord Pronett is just thinking over the message I brought him," Clive told his Captain. "I should give him a little time to consider it before you proceed."

He did not pause for the man to answer and then he turned to the Captain of the Royal Barge.

"Her Ladyship and I will be grateful if you would take us back to the Royal Palace as quickly as possible," he said. "We have no wish for there to be any curiosity at the Court as to why we are aboard His Majesty's Royal Barge"

Then he had an inspiration.

"I think as we have come so far, Captain, it would be extremely pleasant both for Lady Alissia and myself if we could first go a little further downstream."

The Captain looked surprised as Clive continued,

"His Majesty will not need his Royal Barge today, and there is nothing I should enjoy more than to sail in a ship of this remarkable new class and see its performance instead of merely reading about it."

The Captain laughed.

"I would be delighted to show your Lordship how advanced this ship is. In fact without boasting I can say she's outstanding and there's no other ship afloat to equal her."

"That is exactly what I want to see for myself, and, of course, I can then boast about it to all those who have not had the same opportunity."

The Captain laughed as Clive had intended.

"I'll take you downriver, my Lord, and then back again, unless your Lordship has anywhere else you would care to visit."

"That is very kind of you, Captain, and I know that when I report back to His Majesty, how interested he will be."

As the Captain began giving his orders to his crew, Clive joined Alissia.

Nancy had gone down to the cabin where Freddie was waiting rather nervously.

She was worrying that perhaps Clive had just been concerned to save Alissia and he was not really interested in her future.

Equally she realised that when he had boarded Lord Pronett's ship, it was difficult to think of anything except that she had prevented Lord Pronett from marrying Alissia.

When she had first discovered her mother's plans, she had gone up to her bedroom, thrown herself down on her bed and had cried for a long time.

She did not really know why but from the moment she had first seen Lord Pronett, she had thought he was a very attractive man.

He had danced with her, because her mother had more or less insisted on it and she had found, although she could not explain it to herself she felt strangely attracted to him.

He was very different from the other men she had danced with – perhaps it was because he was so tall, in fact as tall as Clive. His hair was dark and he seemed to her much more handsome than the other men she had met.

126

When he came to call at her mother's request, she listened at the door and she had heard her mother telling Lord Pronett that he was to take Alissia away and marry her.

It was then she felt as if a thousand swords pierced her heart.

Even then, having never been in love, she did not fully realise that she was in love with Lord Pronett.

Then she had witnessed him dragging Alissia away and she knew that they were then to be married when they reached Norfolk.

She was past crying and had not wished to go on living.

How could she bear to stay on day after day at the Royal Palace with her mother and stepfather?

If they left London for the country, there would be no one she wanted to see – there were men at the Palace, of course, but they were nearly all old.

The King was certainly comparatively young and so was Clive, yet neither of them was at all concerned with her.

It was just her mother who had such ambition for her and it came to Nancy as a huge shock that the man her mother was pressuring her into marrying was Clive, the Marquis of Morelanton.

He had never paid any attention to her, but it was not only that, she felt he was too big and overwhelming and his personality was too strong.

If she did marry Clive, she would be swallowed up and no longer be herself.

'I don't want to be a Marchioness,' she told herself. 'It is not the title that matters, but the man behind it.'

She knew instinctively that he was not interested in her, even though he had danced several times with her and was very polite when he did so.

"I will be eternally grateful to your stepfather," he had said, "and, of course, to Nanny and Alissia who saved me from the Cromwellians."

"What would they have done to you if they had found you?" Nancy had asked him.

"I would have been thrown into prison and perhaps executed. Then they would have confiscated my house and estate and I would in point of fact have been better dead than alive."

Nancy had heard from Nanny a thousand times how she had disguised him.

"The Cromwellians must have been very stupid," she commented when Clive talked about it.

"I was much younger then," he remarked, "hardly more than a boy and it was undoubtedly Alissia's curls that convinced them that I was a young woman in bed sleeping peacefully."

"You must have been very scared."

"As I was a man, I did not admit to it, but I never tell a lie if I can help it."

It was only when he talked to her about the past and how he had been saved by the ingenuity of both Nanny and Alissia, that he seemed at all human and actually addressed her as a real person.

Otherwise she was just another young girl finding the Royal Palace full of old and rather decrepit people.

'I would so like to be with young gentlemen,' she had thought, 'of my own age, who would laugh and talk to me and perhaps tell me they love me.'

Whenever she had danced with Lord Pronett, she thought he was much easier to talk to than Clive.

He did seem to understand her when she told him how she would like to climb trees or swim, not in the

Thames which was too frightening, but in a small lake that was not too deep.

"I have one like that at my home," he volunteered, "and I used to swim in it in the summer, but there was no one to swim with me, so I was very lonely."

Now she was wondering, as he would no longer be taking Alissia to his home, if she might go in her place.

Perhaps she would swim in his lake with him and he would tell her about all the pictures he owned.

She admitted to herself that she knew nothing about pictures except that some of them were very pretty and it would be so exciting if Lord Pronett would explain to her why they were so significant.

All this passed through her mind as she went down below to the cabin where he was waiting.

But it was not what she expected.

Lord Pronett was standing with his back to her and gazing out of the porthole.

She closed the door gently behind her, but he did not move.

And then she murmured,

"Lord Morelanton – told me I was to come – with you while he takes Alissia back to the Royal Palace."

There was silence before Lord Pronett answered,

"I suppose he also told you that I have made a fool of myself."

Nancy shook her head.

"No, he did not, and I am sure it is something you have never done."

"Why should you be so sure?" he asked without turning round.

"Because you are different from the other people at the Royal Palace who are always wondering if they are saying the right thing and fussing about to be important in the eyes of the King."

Freddie was listening and thought that this was a very strange thing for Nancy to say.

He then turned round and saw her standing near the door.

"I am sorry," she said hesitatingly, "if things have gone wrong for you."

"I think maybe they have gone right, Nancy. I was doing what your mother told me to do and that was a big mistake. How could I have been such a fool as to think that I could marry anyone who did not want to marry me?"

He knew, as he spoke, it was because he was so inexperienced and he was sure that Clive was laughing at him because he had admitted not having made love to any woman.

How could he explain that he had never had the chance?

He had been shut up in a large house with a very old man and a team of elderly servants.

Then as he looked at Nancy he thought that in her own way she was very pretty, not flamboyant, not striking like Barbara Castlemaine or for that matter, Alissia.

But gentle and sweet like the flowers in the spring.

'If I kiss her,' he asked himself, 'I wonder what I would feel?'

Then, as he gazed at her and went on gazing at her, he knew it was something he just had to find out.

CHAPTER SEVEN

Clive walked back to Alissia who, as he reached her, looked at him questioningly.

"It's all right," he told her gently. "We are going back to the Royal Palace, and as I want to talk to you now, I suggest we go down into the cabin."

He guessed as she smiled at him that she had been worried he might insist at the last moment that she should go back to Lord Pronett.

Clive closed the cabin door behind him.

He had changed his mind and told the Captain he should now take them slowly back to the Royal Palace.

"I mean *slowly*," he repeated.

"Thank you! Thank you, Clive," Alissia cried as he came towards her. "I was desperate, but somehow I knew you would save me."

"Just as you once saved me, Alissia," replied Clive. "I think therefore I must now look after you for the rest of your life."

He realised as he spoke that Alissia stiffened.

As she looked up at him there was a question in her eyes.

"I am asking you, Alissia, my darling," he said very quietly, "in a rather roundabout manner *if you will be my wife*."

Alissia gave a gasp.

Then, as he saw a wonderful radiance transform her face, he put his arms round her and pulled her against him.

"I just know I cannot live without you, Alissia."

And then he was kissing her.

As he did so, he realised that it was different from any kiss he had ever given or received in his life.

Her lips were deliciously soft, innocent and very sweet and they were giving him feelings and emotions he had never experienced before.

It was a wonder beyond words, an ecstasy that until now had always eluded him.

Yet he had known he would find it one day.

He kissed her until the Royal Barge suddenly rolled as it turned round against the current.

Then he sat down on the sofa and pulled her close against him again.

"I love you so very much, my darling," he sighed deeply.

He had never really been able to say these magical words before to any woman.

"And I have loved you ever since you rode away in disguise," Alissia whispered to him. "I prayed and prayed then that you would be safe on your long journey North and I have prayed for you ever since."

"That is what you must go on doing, Alissia. I do know, my dearest, we will be very very happy together."

Alissia made a little sound which was almost a sob before she mumbled,

"I thought that this would never happen."

"But you wanted it to?"

"Yes, I wanted it, of course, I wanted you to love me," Alissia answered. "But I thought there were so many beautiful women in the Court that you would never notice me now I have grown up."

"I have thought of you a million times since I left your house in Worcestershire carrying your beautiful curls in my pocket. They have always been with me and have brought me even more luck that you brought me then."

"It is something I will always try to do," Alissia breathed, "and I cannot believe that you really want me to be your wife."

She looked up at Clive and he saw a flicker of fear in her eyes – fear that this beautiful moment which seemed so perfect would prove to be only an illusion.

"I tell you what we will do," he suggested softly. "We will get married *immediately*."

Alissia gave a gasp.

"I can see you are worrying in case I have second thoughts, my darling. Also you are dreading, as I am, the fuss and commotion there will be when the Court knows there is to be a wedding."

Clive paused before he added,

"Doubtless your stepmother will be disagreeable because I am marrying you and not Nancy."

"That certainly is true, but, Clive, just how can we be married – secretly?"

She hesitated over the words as if she thought that she was being presumptuous even to think of such a thing.

Clive smiled.

"If I am going to look after you for the rest of your life, you have to trust me, my darling. What I am going to do is to tell the King in strictest confidence and I know that he will be really delighted at our news.

"He will be the only one to be told of our wedding, and he will help me in arranging for it to take place in his Private Chapel."

Alissia was listening to him wide-eyed.

Then he carried on,

"After that, my precious darling, I am going to take you in this Royal Barge – or whichever one His Majesty will lend us – to my ancestral Castle in Scotland. We will spend our honeymoon there. And then when everyone has become used to the idea of us being married, we will return to London."

"I don't believe it. Am I dreaming this and when I wake up I will find I am alone in my bed? Or perhaps still a prisoner of the dreadful Lord Pronett!"

"He is happy because he is going to marry Nancy, who will suit him far better than you. You are too clever, my darling, not to have ideas and thoughts of your own. But I am quite sure that Nancy will think whatever Lord Pronett thinks and will agree to everything he suggests."

"But do you not want me to do the same for you?"

She was teasing him and Clive gave a laugh.

"I expect that we will argue over many things. But what is all-important is that you love me as I love you and nothing could be more wonderful than that."

"*Nothing*! Nothing!" cried Alissia. "Oh, please my dear wonderful Clive, let's do it your way and as quickly as possible, before anyone finds out that Nancy is missing and starts to search for her."

"I expect your stepmother," Clive smiled somewhat cynically, "will think up a perfectly good explanation for her absence, but your father is more likely to be perturbed about you."

"Papa will be terribly hurt if he is not present at my wedding and we must tell him what has happened before we go to your Castle in Scotland."

"Yes, of course we will," he agreed. "Leave it to me and all you have to do, my precious darling, is to trust me and love me."

He kissed her before she could answer.

And he continued kissing her until he realised that the ship was slowing down and they must now be nearing the Royal Palace.

"I want you to stay here, my darling Alissia," he suggested, as they docked at Whitehall, "while I go ashore and make all the arrangements. If I take a long time, you are not to be frightened – "

"I know I trust you," answered Alissia, "and please, dearest wonderful Clive, remember I have nothing to wear except what I am standing up in."

"I have thought of that too, Alissia, and I will think of every detail of what you will need for our wedding, just as I will guard you for the rest of our lives together."

"I love you, I adore you," sighed Alissia. "You are the most marvellous man in the whole world and I cannot believe that you really love me."

"I will make sure you do once you are my wife – "

He kissed her again.

Then as he heard the gangway being secured, he left the cabin and closed the door behind him.

Alissia put her hands up to her face.

She could hardly believe that what had happened to her was true.

Yet her whole body was pulsating with the wonder and excitement of it all.

'I just adore him and I have always loved him,' she told herself. 'And thank you, thank you, God, for making him love *me*.'

It really was a miracle, she thought, that Clive had been able to save her from such an appalling fate – and that Nancy had been there to tell him what had happened.

She hoped that Nancy would be as happy with Lord Pronett as she herself would be with Clive.

At any rate she was sure that Nancy would be much happier and certainly more sure of herself when she was well away from her mother's far from benign influence.

The Countess had always ordered Nancy about and Alissia had felt for her.

Now Nancy would have to think for herself and the man she married.

Alissia was sure that under these circumstances she would gradually become a very different person.

After giving instructions to the Captain that no one was to board the Royal Barge until he had returned, Clive went straight to see His Majesty the King.

He hurried through the Royal Palace to the King's Private Apartments.

The King was just finishing breakfast and when he saw Clive he rose to his feet.

He then suggested they go into a room next door where they could not be overheard.

"What happened, Clive?" the King asked eagerly. "I have been wondering why you had been away so long."

Clive told him briefly how taking Nancy with him, he had commandeered the Royal Barge on the Palace steps.

And how they had overtaken Lord Pronett's ship by a superb effort on the part of the Royal oarsmen.

"I am sure the Captain enjoyed having something positive to do," the King chuckled.

"He was in his element, Sire."

Then Clive proceeded to tell the King how he had meant to thrash Lord Pronett and teach him a lesson, but instead of which he had felt sorry for him.

The King listened intently to every word and when Clive told him that he intended to marry Alissia he clapped his hands enthusiastically.

"Exactly what I wanted for you, Clive," he cried. "She is lovely, quite outstandingly beautiful and therefore precisely the wife you should have."

Clive smiled.

"You could not pay me a higher compliment, Sire, but actually I now need your help – "

There was nothing the King enjoyed more, now that he was King, than helping other people.

For years he had had to be beholden to those both in England and France who had helped him and at times he had found it very difficult to continue being subserviently grateful.

Now he really wanted to give rather than take and it delighted him to feel that he was powerful enough and rich enough to do so.

"Tell me what you want, Clive," he asked eagerly.

"I would wish to be married to Alissia very quickly here in Your Majesty's Private Chapel with just you there as my Best Man, if you would be so gracious as to do so, Sire, and it would be very kind to ask Lord Dalwaynnie to give away his daughter.

"But it is essential that no one else should be aware of our marriage until we have left for Scotland and it would be delightful if we could possibly spend the first night of our married life in one of Your Majesty's Palaces."

The King laughed.

"I know exactly what you are thinking about and of course you must surely go to Hampton Court, then without anyone knowing you can leave early the next morning for Scotland."

There was a little pause and then as Clive waited, the King added,

"I suppose you want my Royal Barge too?"

"I was too polite to say so, Sire – "

"You know perfectly well that the choice is yours, Clive, and as I have three of them, you can take the one you have just been sailing in, if you like, as it is the most comfortable."

"You are most generous, Sire. I think if you send for Lord Dalwaynnie under some pretext or other that will not cause his wife to be inquisitive, we could be married at noon. Then if we leave for Hampton Court Palace whilst everyone else is having their luncheon, we should be able to avoid the nosey-parkers who will be furious at missing anything as exciting as a wedding in the Royal Palace!"

Clive knew that the way he put it would appeal to the King and it was something he could organise himself.

He had walked in danger for so long that he was a past master at concealing from others what he did not want them to know.

"Now what we have to do," suggested the King, "is to think this all out very seriously. As you propose, Clive, when people are at luncheon they will not be looking out for surprises."

He paused as if he was carefully thinking out the whole scenario, then went on,

"Naturally we don't want them all rushing down to Hampton Court just on the off chance that you might be there."

"God forbid," Clive muttered.

"Or because they guess without us saying anything that something is going on about which they have not been alerted."

Clive guessed he was referring to the equerries who were always hovering in attendance and who believed it was their job not only to look after the King but to think for him.

"Please work it out, Sire, I am sure Your Majesty will do it far better than I can."

"We have both had sufficient experience over the years in subterfuge to know one is always vulnerable to the enemy," replied the King. "In this case that is undoubtedly the Countess, although we must give her credit for bringing you to your senses over Alissia."

Clive looked at him in surprise.

The King smiled.

"I felt from the first time I saw her, that not only was she very beautiful, but you were the only gentleman good enough for anyone so charming and so intelligent."

There was a twisted smirk on his lips as he added,

"I would have pursued her myself, if my hands had not been overfull already!"

Clive chuckled.

"I should have found it difficult in that case to fight you for her. Although I think, Sire, we are very likely to be on equal terms if it comes to duelling or fisticuffs!"

"I am thankful I do not have to experience either with you as my opponent, Clive, as tennis is bad enough when you beat me!

"But now let us get down to brass-tacks. I think it would be wise if we did not tell Lord Dalwaynnie until the very last minute."

"I would certainly agree, Sire."

"In fact, Clive, I think the very best way would be to send an equerry to tell him I want him to have luncheon with me, but that he should come early at midday since I want to ask his advice about some current issue."

"That is an excellent idea, Sire. The Countess will undoubtedly think Your Majesty wants to ask his advice on your pictures or perhaps there is to be a meeting of experts to discuss improvements to the Palace."

"That is exactly what I thought myself."

There was a short pause before Clive said,

"Yet another problem is that Alissia has nothing to wear but what she now has on. She cannot risk collecting her clothes from her Apartment for obvious reasons."

The King laughed.

"I should have thought of that one myself, knowing how women fuss continually about their appearance!"

"Well, it's a good long way to Scotland, Sire, and just one gown is not particularly suitable for such a long voyage."

The King held up his hand.

"Now just don't disturb me, Clive, I am thinking. I suppose there is someone we can trust in the Dalwaynnie Apartment?"

"There is someone who I should like to come with us to help look after my wife, Sire, and to whom I owe a deep debt of gratitude."

The King had heard the story before.

"You mean Nanny?"

Clive nodded.

"Very well, Clive, she must be informed at once. Are you going to tell her – or shall I?"

The King was only teasing and Clive added,

"If you are now thinking of going in disguise and knocking on the back door, I am afraid you might not act the part sufficiently well not to be exposed!"

"Very well then, Clive. What do you suggest?"

"I think I should write a note to Nanny and have it delivered to her by my valet who I trust. They could both then collect all Alissia's clothes and smuggle them out of the Apartment without anyone noticing their movements."

"I hope you are right," sighed the King, "but as you know the Palace is stocked with eyes that see too much and ears that are listening to every flutter of the wind."

"A perfect description!" exclaimed Clive, "which will undoubtedly go down in history one way or another!"

Both men laughed and then the King suggested,

"Now I intend to send for my Chaplain and I think it would be a mistake for him to see you or to know your name until the Marriage Service is actually taking place, and therefore I would propose that you now go back to your future wife."

"I will do that, Sire, but when will we meet Your Majesty again? I am sure it would be dangerous for me to come to this room and then have to walk some distance to the Chapel."

"Then we will meet outside the Chapel at exactly a quarter-to-one, Clive. I will have with me – God willing – Alissia's father, and no one will have the slightest idea that anything unusual is about to take place."

"Amen to that, Sire."

Clive then left the King's Apartments and went to his own that was actually not very far away.

When he arrived, he wrote a letter to Nanny making it as brief as possible.

He next told his faithful valet, who he had brought from Scotland, that he was now on a secret mission.

The man had been with Clive since he had arrived home after the Battle of Worcester and was very obviously elated at the whole idea.

"That'll be somethin' new, my Lord," he remarked cheerfully.

"It is not only a secret, but it is absolutely essential that you do without question exactly all I ask you to do and without anyone except Nanny, who you know, being aware that anything is afoot."

"Your Lordship can trust me," replied Angus.

"I know that I can, Angus, but you will have to be extremely clever about it. The things I have asked Nanny in this note to provide have to be transferred secretly to the Royal Barge, which will be waiting at the further entrance on the Embankment immediately below the Palace."

"I knows the one you mean, my Lord."

"I am going on a voyage," Clive went on, "and I will need my clothes with me as well."

"Am I comin' with Your Lordship?" Angus asked.

"I think you had better do so, otherwise you will find it very difficult to keep the voyage a secret from those who will doubtless agitate to find out where we are going once we have left the Royal Palace."

He saw that Angus was thrilled with the secret – he already felt certain that his Master was eloping with some lovely lady or else involved in some daredevil escapade which at all costs must be kept from the nosey-parkers who surrounded the King.

After a few more instructions Angus went off with his note for Nanny.

Clive then walked as nonchalantly as he could to the Embankment.

The Royal Barge where Alissia was waiting for him had not moved since he had left it.

The Captain, on his instructions, had given orders that no one was to come aboard before he, Clive, returned.

As soon as Clive then stepped onto the gangway, the Captain of the Royal Barge, who had been looking out for him all this time, came hurrying towards him.

"Is everything all right, my Lord?" he asked Clive cautiously.

"His Majesty was most pleased, Captain, with the way you carried out what he knew to be a difficult task."

The Captain almost blushed.

"His Majesty," Clive then continued, "considers it important that no one knows what has occurred and that the ship we left behind at the mouth of the Thames is not mentioned in any way at the Royal Palace."

"I'll see that His Majesty's instructions are carried out and I'll inform my crew at once," the Captain replied stoutly.

"What I would now like, Captain, is to have a look at your Master Suite, and to know if you will be ready in two hours time to take us to Hampton Court Palace and to then leave at first light tomorrow morning, without anyone being aware of it, for Scotland."

He saw the Captain's eyes light up at the idea of a long voyage.

Clive realised that the King's staff on duty at the Royal Palace found the lack of activity extremely boring – he himself had suggested there should be races amongst the Royal Barges to last over two or three weeks to keep the men happy.

"There is, however, one further condition," Clive added. "That is that we don't tell your oarsmen that we are leaving until the voyage has started. They must have no idea until we are actually at sea that we are not returning to London for some considerable time."

The Captain did not hesitate.

He promised that his men would not be informed of their destination and that he would not even tell his junior Officers that they were leaving London.

Clive knew that the majority of the men on board who had been signed on as oarsmen were not married and they therefore had no particular commitment ashore.

In the meantime he did appreciate that the Captain would have to be extremely careful.

He had to bring on board whatever supplies would be needed, in particular sufficient food and water, without attracting attention.

And it would be a mistake for anyone to question any of this before they had actually left for Scotland.

After he had finished talking with the Captain, he went to the cabin where he had left Alissia.

As he expected, she had remained in the cabin and had not gone up on deck where she might be seen.

As he entered the cabin, she gave a cry of joy and ran towards him.

"You are back, Clive!" she called out breathlessly. "Is everything all right?"

"Everything is fine, my darling. We are going to be married a little before one o'clock in the King's Private Chapel. I have arranged for your father to give you away, while His Majesty will be my Best Man. No one else will have the slightest idea what is taking place until we are too far away to hear them making a fuss about it."

"You are so very very clever," Alissia sighed. "It would spoil everything if my Stepmama tried to stop us or made one of her dreadful scenes. Or if all those people at Court came rushing at us, which I know you would hate."

"You have to look after me just as I have to look after you," Clive smiled, "and I can imagine nothing I will enjoy more."

He then kissed her.

And it was a long time later before they were able to talk about anything again.

Finally Angus came aboard with Alissia's clothes.

When she saw that they were all in bags that were normally used for the laundry, she laughed.

"No one were a bit interested in me carryin' these along the corridors," Angus explained, "but they would've questioned where I were a-goin' if I'd brought them in a trunk!"

"Yes, of course they would" Alissia cried. "It was very clever of you and Nanny to conceal my clothes so brilliantly."

"There be a helluva lot more to come, includin' his Lordship's," Angus told her. "Nanny told me to get back as quick as I could."

"And Nanny must always be obeyed, I have known that ever since I could crawl!"

"Nanny be ever so excited to be comin' with you, my Lady, but she didn't tell me where we be a-goin'."

"I am sure his Lordship will do that when you see him," giggled Alissia.

When Nanny came aboard at exactly twelve-thirty, Alissia then quickly changed her day dress for one that was completely white.

It was a dress she had never worn before and she had bought it because it was so pretty and as it happened, Nanny had said to her on its arrival from the dressmakers,

"It looks so like one of them weddin' gowns to me, dearie. Are you hopin' it'll come in useful?"

"Of course I am," replied Alissia, "but I only hope I don't have to wait until it goes out of fashion!"

She had been speaking jokingly to Nanny.

But at the same time it did pass through her mind that the only gentleman at Court she would really like to marry would be Clive, although so far he had paid little attention to her.

'But I am going to marry him,' she told herself, 'and this gown is exactly what I want him to see me in on our wedding day.'

There was no wedding veil amongst her clothes, but she found some tulle which she knew would be even more becoming than a heavy veil – but she would not put it on until she entered the Chapel itself.

Angus went backwards and forwards conveying the clothes, laundry bag after laundry bag.

On his last journey he brought Jimbo back with him and two spaniels belonging to Clive.

Alissia gave a cry of delight.

"How could we go without them?" she asked.

At twenty minutes to one Clive came on board and knocked on her door.

She had not moved outside the cabin where Nanny was arranging her clothes, just in case she might be seen by anyone looking out of the windows of the Royal Palace.

Now when she saw Clive, she gave a loud cry of astonishment.

He was dressed in his kilt, sporran and plaid and she thought he had never looked so smart or attractive as he did in all his Highland regalia.

"I didn't think you would be married dressed as a Scotsman," she told him.

"Which is what I am, Alissia, and therefore I am hoping that I will not be recognised as we skip through the corridors to the Chapel!"

"I hope I will be smart enough for you," Alissia asked him, slight doubt creeping into voice.

"You look as lovely as I am sure you expect me to tell you, and I promise that I will say it a thousand times more once we are married."

Nanny came bustling in from the other cabin.

"Thank you, Nanny," said Clive, "for coming with us. We could not mange without you."

"I should think not," replied Nanny. "I've looked after her Ladyship since she was born, as I once looked after you, and it'd be a real sad day if you *could* manage without me."

Clive laughed and reassured her,

"I promise you we will never do that."

He took Alissia ashore at a quarter-to-one and they knew that by the time they reached the King's Apartment her father would be with him.

Clive looked to see if the King's Private Chaplain was in the Chapel and then he knocked on the door of the King's sitting room.

He noticed as he did so that the King's equerry who usually sat beside the door had been sent away and there appeared to be no one in the Private Apartments except themselves.

He heard the King call out,

"Come in."

As they walked in Alissia ran towards her father.

"My darling daughter," he cried. "His Majesty told me exactly what has been happening and I am exceedingly grateful to Clive for having saved you. And I am delighted and thrilled that you are marrying the one man I would have chosen for you had you asked me to do so."

Alissia having curtsied low to the King, kissed her father.

Then the King suggested,

"I feel so involved in this wedding that I am going to call Clive and Alissia, '*A Royal love match*'."

And next he smiled broadly,

"Come on. Let us get it over with and the married couple can be off to Hampton Court."

"Is that where you are going after the Marriage Service?" Alissia's father asked Clive.

"Only for the one night and then we are going to Scotland. We will, of course, write to you from there and tell you when we are coming South again."

"I cannot spare you for too long," the King insisted. "For the simple reason that I will want to play tennis with you, Clive. Everyone else I play with I can beat too easily, so you must come back as quickly as possible to prevent me from becoming too proud of myself!"

They all laughed.

And then they walked into the Chapel.

Alissia had put on her veil and now she slipped her arm through her father's.

The Marriage Service was short but inspiring.

The Chaplain was an old man who made the words seem to have a special meaning for the two people making their vows in the sight of God.

When he gave the Blessing, Alissia felt certain that her mother was near her, making sure that her daughter would be as happy as she had been with her father.

There was the best mulled wine waiting for them in the King's sitting room.

When the King had drunk their health, they hurried down the stairs to the Embankment and the Royal Barge.

Lord Dalwaynnie then joined the luncheon party, which had been the excuse to deceive the Countess.

It had all been planned so carefully and in minute detail.

Clive and Alissia ran up the gangway together and were piped aboard and the Royal Barge began to move out into the Thames as soon as they were safely on board.

Alissia was absolutely certain that no one had the slightest idea that a very important marriage had just taken place secretly in the Royal Palace.

The King had made arrangements for their stay at Hampton Court Palace to be secret.

The Royal Apartments had been opened for them and the King had emphasised in the letter he had sent to the Officials in charge of the Palace that no one outside was to be told they were present.

There were cascades of flowers in the sitting room and the bedroom.

They had enjoyed luncheon on the Royal Barge on the way to Hampton Court and then, as they were to leave early the next morning, Clive ordered dinner to be served at seven-thirty.

Because Alissia had never been to Hampton Court Palace before, they spent most of the afternoon exploring the many rooms.

She admired all the beautiful pictures, furniture and the Palace itself.

To her surprise Clive knew the whole story.

"I have always been very interested in Palaces," he explained, "and Hampton Court has a special history of its own that has always intrigued me."

After dinner was over and Clive had proposed a toast to their future happiness, Nanny helped Alissia into the bed which had held so many Kings and Queens in the past.

Nanny paused at the door and turned.

"You look so lovely, dearie," she said as she looked back. "May God bless you and give you endless happiness for ever and ever."

Alissia looked very small in the great bed.

Yet with the heavy curtains on each side of it and her golden hair falling over the pillows, she looked, as her bridegroom was to think, as if she had stepped straight out of a fairy story.

Clive came into the bedroom very quietly through the communicating door.

As he walked towards the bed, Alissia put out her arms towards him.

"I still cannot believe this is really happening," she murmured. "I still think I must be dreaming."

"I have felt the same all day," replied Clive. "You realise, my darling, that we have won a great victory on our own. You and I have found each other and that is the most important achievement of all, nothing and no one can spoil for me the wonder of knowing that you are my wife and no one will ever take you from me."

Alissia could find no words to say.

She just looked up at him.

She had a rapt expression in her eyes he had never seen in any woman's.

It was not just ordinary love.

It was a love that was Holy and perfect.

And he knew it came from a beautiful girl who had never even been kissed by another man.

She was his – all his – completely and absolutely.

As she had been, although he had not been aware of it, since he had left her in the nursery all those years ago and in spite of incredible dangers he had reached his own Castle in Scotland.

It had all happened in the past.

Now they were starting a new future together.

Tomorrow they would be leaving England.

They would start, as he so wanted, his marriage in his own country and in his own Castle.

Without Alissia's help he might never have seen them again and he would not have been here with her at this magical moment.

He threw off the robe he was wearing and climbed into the bed.

As he put his arms round Alissia and drew her close to him, he thought she was trembling.

"You are not frightened of me, my darling one?" he asked her tenderly.

"No. I am only so excited and it is so wonderful that I am still afraid I may wake up and find it all a dream," Alissia whispered.

"Then I will make sure that you don't wake up – "

He bent his head and kissed her very gently.

As he went on kissing her, each moment becoming more possessive and more passionate, he felt as if her soft body melted into his.

"I love you. I adore you," Alissia was saying.

Clive repeated the words and he knew as he did so that the ecstatic love they had found was something he had searched for for thousands of years.

It was the love that came from God and which had, through all Alissia's prayers, brought them both to safety together.

"You are mine, mine," he breathed as he kissed her.

When he made her his, he knew that they had both entered a special Heaven of their own.

A Heaven that had been waiting for them ever since they were born.

Which by the mercy of God they had found at last and would never lose.

"I love you, Clive."

"I love you, Alissia."

The words kept repeating themselves until locked in each other's arms they fell into a blissful sleep.